**'It's good to know you don't ha[ve]
a problem with a woman being in
charge.'**

'This is a one time and one time only deal. My
tolerance and acceptance will only stretch so far.
Once I'm back on my feet again you'd be unwise
to push any advantage you gained while I was
laid up.'

Raising her brows, Kit responded smartly, 'When
you're back on your feet again you'll no longer
need my services, so such a possibility won't
even arise. I'll be looking after another client…
hopefully one a little less egotistical than you.'

Worryingly, any response he normally might
have made to such an unflattering observation
deserted Hal. The idea that Kit was already
eagerly contemplating a new client—one 'a little
less egotistical' than he was—seriously bothered
him.

But he couldn't help but notice how her smooth
alabaster cheeks had a faintly scarlet tint to them.
How interesting, he thought. Perhaps it wasn't
just his 'egotistical' nature that ruffled the coolly
efficient redhead?

'You're blushing, Ms Blessington. Does it disturb
you to get [   ]ause if it
doe[   ]nage
wh[   ]ted.

The day **Maggie Cox** saw the film version of *Wuthering Heights*, with a beautiful Merle Oberon and a very handsome Laurence Olivier, was the day she became hooked on romance. From that day onwards she spent a lot of time dreaming up her own romances, secretly hoping that one day she might become published and get paid for doing what she loved most! Now that her dream is being realised, she wakes up every morning and counts her blessings. She is married to a gorgeous man, and is the mother of two wonderful sons. Her two other great passions in life—besides her family and reading/writing—are music and films.

Recent titles by the same author:

IN PETRAKIS'S POWER
WHAT HIS MONEY CAN'T HIDE
DISTRACTED BY HER VIRTUE
A DEVILISHLY DARK DEAL

THE TYCOON'S DELICIOUS DISTRACTION

BY
MAGGIE COX

Published in Great Britain 2014
by Mills & Boon, an imprint of Harlequin (UK) Limited,
Eton House, 18-24 Paradise Road, Richmond, Surrey, TW9 1SR

© 2014 Maggie Cox

ISBN: 978 0 263 90816 9

Harlequin (UK) Limited's policy is to use papers that are natural, renewable and recyclable products and made from wood grown in sustainable forests. The logging and manufacturing processes conform to the legal environmental regulations of the country of origin.

Printed and bound in Spain
by Blackprint CPI, Barcelona

THE TYCOON'S
DELICIOUS
DISTRACTION

To the lovely Maddie
who is the bravest and wittiest girl I know!

CHAPTER ONE

IN A FIT of pique, Henry Treverne—Hal to his friends—wheeled himself along the parquet hallway up to the wall panel in the door and buzzed the concierge.

'If anyone else turns up for an interview today tell them I've come down with malaria, will you? I'm done with talking to fawning women who are convinced they can magic my problems away like Cinderella's fairy godmother, and I've also had my fill of the ones that gaze at me like I'm some kind of longed-for early Christmas present!'

'But, Mr Treverne, your next applicant is already here… Do you really think you've got malaria? If that's true, shouldn't you be in the hospital?'

The concierge of Hal's building—a down-to-earth young Londoner called Charlie—sounded understandably perturbed. Hefting a frustrated sigh, Hal tunnelled his fingers through the mane of coal-black hair that was in dire need of a proper cut and bit back a curse.

'Of course I haven't got malaria. I've just got back from Aspen, Colorado, not the damn Amazon!' He brought himself up short. 'What do you mean my next applicant is already here?'

Impatiently unfolding the scrunched-up piece of

paper lying on his lap, he couldn't help but succumb to a ripe curse, when he saw there was one more person the agency had scheduled him to see. A woman named Kit Blessington. God save him from one more insincere female desperate for the chance to be his 'carer' and in all probability make herself a nice little bonus by selling a story about her experience to the press when he was back on his feet again.

'The lady arrived early and is waiting to see you, Mr Treverne.'

'Well, you can tell Ms Blessed, or whatever her name is, that I'm too tired to see anyone else today. Tell her she can come back tomorrow.'

'I'd rather see you now, if I could, Mr Treverne? After all, that was what was arranged. Plus, it's not convenient for me to come back tomorrow.'

Hal was taken aback by the assertively toned female voice that sounded in his ear. 'What do you mean, it's not convenient?' he growled. 'Are you in the market for a job or are you not?' His already bad mood plummeted even more. The woman clearly hadn't taken him seriously when he'd said he was too tired.

'I wouldn't be signed on with the agency if I wasn't interested in a job, Mr Treverne. And, by the way, my name is Blessington—not Blessed.'

'What's the reason you can't come back tomorrow?' Even as he ground out the question the back of Hal's neck prickled with intense dislike for this woman he hadn't even come face to face with yet.

'If you must know, I have another interview to attend in Edinburgh. I can't see you tomorrow if I'm travelling up to Scotland. That's why I'd like to keep my appointment with you today.'

The frank confession rendered him momentarily dumbstruck. He wasn't best pleased that she'd arranged another interview when she hadn't even given him the courtesy of seeing *him* yet. What did she think she was playing at? Surely the agency must have told her who he was…that under the circumstances he had to be a priority?

'What the hell do you want to go to Scotland for?' he burst out, not caring that he sounded rude and unreasonable.

There was a brief pause, then in a level tone she replied, 'I go wherever the work takes me, Mr Treverne. We don't just work in the UK. The agency sends us all over Europe as well. Now, will you see me today or not?'

Feeling particularly belligerent, because inside the cast his leg was intolerably aching, and itching as well, Hal retorted, 'I'll give you ten minutes, Ms Blessington. Ten minutes should be ample time for me to glean whether you're suitable or not for the position, and whether it would indeed be better if you simply went ahead with your interview in Edinburgh. You'd better come up.'

'Thank you. I appreciate it. But just to reassure you, Mr Treverne, I too quite quickly make up my mind about whether I want to work for someone or not. So, yes…I'm sure it won't take long for either of us to reach a decision.'

She was playing verbal bat and ball with him, Hal realised, and it made him feel as if she was the one taking charge of the situation, not him. It certainly didn't bode well for her interview.

Damn his accident! It beggared belief that he'd surrendered to the crazy impulse to agree to a stupid contest on the ski slopes with his ex-business partner Simon. If his pride hadn't made him take the bait he wouldn't be in the intolerable position he was in now—recovering from a lengthy operation to help repair a badly damaged femur and unable to do all the things he had no doubt taken for granted and shouldn't have.

If he hadn't been in so much pain as the paramedics lifted him onto the stretcher, he would have checked to see if the concern Simon had so loudly expressed to the crowd that had gathered was sincere. *Hal very much doubted it.* He could just imagine the man who had always been his rival describing the scene to mutual colleagues and friends and commenting, *How the mighty are fallen…*

One thing was certain. Hal wasn't going to live down the ignominy of the painful incident any time soon.

Disgruntled and hurting, he punched the keypad to open the door and reversed the wheelchair a couple of feet back down the hall as he waited for the irritatingly forthright Ms Blessington to come in and be interviewed. In truth, he was absolutely prepared to dislike her on sight.

When he first glimpsed the gloriously red hair that rippled down over her slim shoulders as she came through the door he wasn't surprised. *It was said that redheads were feisty and opinionated.* And this particular redhead definitely had the look and stance of a public school head girl. He already knew that she was assertive—a woman who knew what she wanted and wasn't afraid to state it—and the unfussy green wool dress and almost military-style tartan jacket she wore with it suggested she selected her clothes more out of practicality than from any desire to make a fashion statement. The outfit might even have been bought at a charity shop. Yet the bright cerise stockings she'd teamed with sensible brown court shoes hinted at an intriguing rebellious streak that belied the illusion of 'needs must' and definitely gave Hal pause.

Lifting his head, he was momentarily taken aback to find his gaze captured by a pair of the prettiest cornflower-blue eyes he'd ever seen. Even before she opened her mouth to speak he had concluded that the woman was a fascinating conundrum that under more conducive circumstances he might, just *might* be tempted to try and unravel. But when she next spoke any impulse to be more interested than he should be instantly vanished.

'I can see why you sounded so bad-tempered just now.' Frowning, she set a purple velvet shoulder bag down on the floor and purposefully stepped towards him, like an extremely efficient ward nurse intent on taking his temperature. 'If you don't mind my saying so, you do look rather uncomfortable. Your brow is beaded with sweat and I can see you're in pain. They told me at the agency that you'd broken your femur and that it was a bad break. Do you need a painkiller? If you tell me where they are I'll get them for you, if you'd like?'

'I've taken a couple—just a few minutes ago.'

For stupefying seconds the arresting floral scent his redoubtable interviewee wore transported Hal to a beautiful spring garden after a gentle rain had fallen, and it made it hard for him to think straight. It didn't help that she stood close enough for him to reach out and touch one of the fiery red coils of hair that cascaded over her shoulders, and the shockingly inappropriate impulse made his heart thunder inside his chest like a herd of galloping horses.

Taken aback by the surprising reaction, he coughed a little to clear his throat. 'The pills take a while to kick in. So, no, I don't need you to get me any more. The last thing I need is to feel comatose. I think we should just get on with the interview, don't you?'

'Of course.' The redhead's alabaster skin flushed a little, but quickly getting over any embarrassment she might have felt and levelling a searching glance at him, she asked, 'Instead of staying in that wheelchair, would you not prefer to conduct our interview lying on the sofa, with some cushions behind you for a while? I'm sure it would be a lot more comfortable. I can help you, if you'd like?'

'Ms Blessing?'

'Blessington.'

He should have known correction was inevitable, and Hal chewed down on his lip to stop himself from responding with something he might regret.

'Let's get one thing straight. I'm *not* looking to hire a facsimile of Florence Nightingale. I have round-the-clock access to a highly professional medical team if I want it. What I need—that is, the person I'm looking to hire—is someone who can be a temporary companion and help with all things practical while I recuperate. That's why I need a home help. I need someone not just to drive me wherever I want, to arrange for shopping to be delivered, make the odd cup of tea or coffee and rustle up a meal or a snack whenever I need it, but also someone with the ability to make intelligent conversation, who has an interest in music and film—two of the things that entertain me the most. I want this person to be on call twenty-four-seven in case I can't sleep and want some company."

The woman in front of him released the smallest sigh, but Hal didn't think it was because the criteria for the post that he'd outlined in any way daunted her. In fact the interested examination she'd submitted him to as he spoke had been unflinchingly direct.

'That's more or less what the agency told me you needed, Mr Treverne, and I want you to know that I have no problem with any of those things.'

'You've worked for clients with similar requirements before?'

'Yes. I recently worked for an actress recovering from a particularly bad bout of flu that had left her feeling extremely weak. I had to do many of the things you've mentioned for her too, until she could manage on her own again.'

The experience hadn't been a particularly good one for Kit, because the woman in question was spoilt and disagreeable. She had run her ragged for the six long weeks she'd worked for her, taking every opportunity to let her know how much she was admired and envied by her fellow thespians in the theatrical world for her beauty and acting prowess—her tone suggesting that Kit should feel privileged that she'd hired her.

But Kit hadn't felt resentful towards the woman, because she clearly hadn't been able to see how very unattractive her vanity and superior manner actually made her. During all the time Kit had been with her she hadn't had so much as one person call to see how she was doing. Kit had ended up feeling very sorry for her.

'And, seeing as I need you to be available round the clock, you're aware that this is a live-in position?'

Hal's arresting voice broke into her reverie.

'Most of the jobs with the agency *are*. Don't worry—all your requirements were explained to me in detail, Mr Treverne. Is there anything else you'd like to ask me?'

'Yes. How old are you?'

'I'm twenty-six.'

'And you don't have a "significant other" who might express reservations about you living-in? Especially when the person you'll be working for is male?' If Hal had hoped to rattle her with his slightly mocking inflection, he'd failed. His outspoken interviewee gave no visible sign whatsoever that the question had perturbed her in any way. Instead, she remained unshakably composed.

'I'm unattached, so there's no one in my life to express any reservations. In any case I wouldn't tolerate being in a relationship with someone who dictated what I could or couldn't do, or minded that I lived in if it was part of my job…which it clearly is.'

The blunt confession piqued Hal's curiosity even more. He found himself wondering what her story was. His sister Sam, who invariably liked to try and get to the root of someone's make-up, would no doubt presume the woman's outspoken and direct attitude had manifested itself as a result of her being bullied—either during her childhood or even in the recent past. Because of it, she'd probably made a mental decision not to let herself be intimidated by anyone ever again. He could almost hear Sam saying it. In Sam's psychology practice she'd seen plenty of clients with similar stories. Except it wasn't hard to guess that Ms Kit Blessington was no push-over… In Hal's view, only a fool would presume otherwise.

The notion didn't disturb him one jot. He'd rather have someone capable and strong-minded working for him than some shy wallflower who wouldn't say boo to a goose. It took him aback to realise that in the space of a few short minutes he'd become inexplicably fascinated by the woman. Fascinated or not, he reminded himself, it was hardly a good idea for him to be interested in a prospective employee…albeit a temporary one. At any rate, it wasn't a fascination that meant he was remotely attracted to her, he assured himself sternly. She might be unquestionably pretty, but she was no knock-out that he'd have trouble resisting should he hire her.

As if to remind him of the reason for them having this discussion at all, his leg started to throb like the blazes, and once again a wave of perspiration beaded his forehead. *Should he or shouldn't he give her a few days' trial to see if she was suitable?* God knew none of the other applicants he'd seen had been remotely suitable. Damn it, he needed someone capable and reliable to help him out as soon as possible or he'd be fit to be tied! His situation had already begun making him feel unbearably imprisoned, and for a man who was used to being so active—living life at 'breakneck speed', as his sister so often observed with concern—the experience was bordering on *torture*…

Giving the redhead a long, assessing glance, he said, 'Follow me into the living room and we can talk about this some more.' Hal's tone rang with the innate command that came only too easily to him. Would his potential home help be able to handle an often belligerent and exacting male who made no apology for it?

'You mean you want the interview to continue?'

'Well, I'm not inviting you into my living room to

get your opinion on the decor, Ms Blessington.' Even as he uttered the droll reply Hal registered that it was the first time he'd seen so much as a flicker of doubt in the woman's bright blue eyes—as if she'd momentarily feared her forthright manner might have talked her out of the job. As he turned away to steer the wheelchair further down the hall towards the living room he couldn't help mentally storing the information in case he ever had occasion to draw upon it. In his profession he'd long ago learned the wisdom of knowing his advantages when it came to relationships—professional or otherwise. And neither was he above using them...

Following behind the wheelchair, Kit used the time to further examine the man tagged as 'Lucky Henry' in the music business. Apparently, according to people in the know, he had the enviable gift of discovering potentially lucrative talent and backing it financially, expanding that talent even more, and obviously making himself even richer and more successful in the process as the artists he sponsored made platinum sales on their records and became the 'next big thing' in the pop industry.

Even though she didn't have the slightest desire to experience how the other half lived in that shallow, materialistic world—a world that in her opinion could only breed disappointment and unhappiness when an artist's star began to wane and they were no longer 'flavour of the month'—Kit couldn't deny she had often been intrigued as to what happened to the budding stars who *didn't* make it.

And, more than that, she was indisputably interested as to the motivation behind Henry Treverne's decision to become an impresario in such a dog-eat-dog profession. Having been a temporary home help to many celebrity clients, she'd done her research and learned that 'Lucky Henry' came from landed gentry and had grown up with every possible material advantage. Was money and success the only thing that inspired him because he'd already experienced being raised with the proverbial silver spoon in his mouth? *Surely the man must be a more complex character than his public persona suggested?*

Not only had he enjoyed every material advantage growing up, he was also blessed with an extraordinary physique and arresting good looks to boot. As Kit's gaze settled on broad, athletic shoulders in a cream cashmere sweater and thick dark hair curling somewhat rebelliously over the neckline she couldn't help wondering that if he should offer her the job, and if she accepted it, perhaps this time she really would be biting off more than she could chew. She might have deliberately given Henry Treverne the impression that she wasn't particularly concerned about whether he gave her the job or not because she'd already lined up another interview in Edinburgh, but the truth was it *did* matter to Kit—because the agency was paying the highest possible rate for this position and, as well as looking good on her résumé, it would really help boost her savings—savings she was eager to add to so that she might at long last buy the little bolthole she'd always yearned for.

'What's Kit short for?'

The question was fired at her as they reached the living room. Not answering immediately, Kit glanced round to get her bearings. The first thing that hit her was the bold oil painting of a man scaling what looked to be the sheer face of a glacier. Something about the tilt of the head, along with the colour of his hair and the breadth of his shoulders, made Kit realise that the daredevil mountaineer was Henry. Transfixed, it was hard for her to look away.

'That's you, isn't it?' she said.

His tight-lipped expression told her the question unsettled him.

'It is.'

Ignoring the opportunity to comment further—unlike most men, who notoriously loved to brag about their daring exploits—he remained stubbornly uncommunicative, so she returned her attention to the living room. She'd guessed his taste would veer towards the contemporary and she was right. The high-quality monochrome furniture that predominated was ultra-chic, with smooth clean lines, and it was arranged almost like a display of elite sculptures at an exhibition. Even though it had probably cost and arm and a leg to furnish, it was hardly the most inviting living room Kit had ever been in… However, the three streamlined ebony leather couches that took centre stage were strewn with brightly coloured Moroccan-style silk cushions that made her think he must have surrendered to a rogue impulse to inject some warmth into the arrangement.

'Kit is short for Katherine, and Katherine is spelt with a K.' Breaking off her reverie, she returned to his question regarding her name.

Her answer was the one she usually gave when quizzed about it. Her mother had been very particular about the spelling…it was the one decision in her life she'd appeared to have made with ease. *It was a far from a normal occurrence.* When it came to making informed decisions for herself and her daughter Elizabeth Blessington reacted to the task like a billiard ball run amok—decisions were random and precarious. How could they not be when they were invariably emotionally driven rather than made using reason and common sense? That was why Kit had found herself taking charge from such a ridiculously young age. While her friends had been playing with dolls or games Kit had usually been sitting in her mother's kitchen, trying to help find some practical solution to her latest dramatic dilemma—or if not that then consoling her because some unsuitable man she'd become infatuated with had once again let her down.

Elizabeth Blessington's choice of men had been disastrous, and the self-destructive pattern had begun with Kit's father. Ralph Cottonwood had been a genuine Romany gypsy who had selfishly abandoned Elizabeth when she'd become pregnant. In her mother's wistful words, 'He couldn't be tied down to a conventional married life when the allure of the open road would always call to him.'

Although Kit had missed not having a steady male influence in her life, she'd long ago decided that her itinerant father had probably done her and her mother a favour by not sticking around. One totally impractical parent with her head in the clouds had been quite enough to cope with...

'Why don't you sit down?'

Moving his wheelchair into the centre of the room, Henry vaguely waved his hand towards the couches.

'Okay.' As she settled herself Kit rested her hands together in her lap and patiently waited for him to continue. *A sudden realisation struck her.* She'd thought his eyes were green, but in the beam of gold sunlight that streamed through the windows she saw that they were a chameleon-like hazel, and fringed with enviably lustrous long black lashes. She'd have to be made of stone not to admire such a compelling visage…

'So tell me, Katherine with a K, what impulse led you into doing this kind of work?'

'I decided to do it because I like helping people.'

'And what qualifications do you have?'

The question didn't faze her, even though she'd often regretted her lack of opportunity to study for a profession. But with a mother who was often in financial trouble because she didn't have a clue how to manage money Kit had had no choice but to start work at sixteen so that she could contribute to the household income and help pay the rent.

'Do you mean professional qualifications?'

He nodded.

Pursing her lips for a moment, Kit quickly gathered her thoughts. 'I've done some fairly intensive first-aid training courses and completed a carer's certificate. But what I lack in professional qualifications I make up for by having plenty of "hands-on" experience in helping to take care of people. If you speak to Barbara—the manager at the agency—she'll clarify what I've said. I've been with her for the past five years and my record is exemplary. The agency standards are extremely high, and she wouldn't keep me on if I didn't help her live up to that.'

Her heart was thudding a little as she finished speaking, because Henry's expression had at first been perturbed and then somewhat amused. *Was he perhaps thinking she must be crazy if she thought he'd seriously consider taking on someone with minimal qualifications to work for him?* Kit hoped he would at least give her a chance to demonstrate her competence. Inexplicably, the thought of travelling up to Scotland tomorrow had strangely lost its appeal.

'It's lucky for you that I'm a risk-taker. Other people might call it reckless, but fortunately I don't much care what other people think. Okay, Ms Blessington, when can you start?'

He was going to give her a chance? Secretly elated, but careful not to show it, Kit strove for her usual composure. 'Are you saying that you'd like to offer me the job, Mr Treverne?'

He immediately combed his fingers through his unruly dark hair and scowled. 'Isn't that why you're here… because you want to work for me?'

'Yes, I am. But—'

'Firstly, don't call me Mr Treverne. It's far too formal. You can call me Hal. I'm sure you can guess that's not an invitation I extend to many, but for the purpose of ease of communication I'm extending it to you, Kit. And, yes…I'm offering you the job and I'd like you to start tomorrow. My sister assures me that the agency you work for does indeed have a good reputation for employing reliable and competent people—people who know how to employ discretion and respect confidentiality. That's especially important for businessmen in the public eye like me, as I'm sure you're aware? And, by the way, there's a confidentiality clause in the contract that I'll need to get you to sign. I trust you're okay with that?'

'Of course.'

Emitting a relieved sigh, Hal nodded. 'Then you can arrive tomorrow, just after breakfast. Depending on what kind of night I've had, I usually endeavour to have toast and coffee at around eight. There's one more thing…I have an appointment at the hospital at ten. You'll have to drive me.' Looking thoughtful, he paused, narrowing his chameleon-like gaze. 'I presume you'd like to accept the position?'

'Yes…yes, I would.' Rising to her feet, Kit walked towards him, her smile perhaps a little more cautious than usual. Henry Treverne was a commandingly attractive man and she wouldn't be truthful if she didn't privately admit that it worried her. It had never happened before but she'd often feared that if she fell for a man she worked for it would be the ruination of all her dreams and plans. Add to that the fact that he was still very much an unknown quantity with regard to what he would be like as an employer, she sensed, going by his brusque manner, that she would have her work cut out in proving to him he'd chosen the right person for the job.

'Thank you…thank you so much. I promise I won't let you down.'

'I sincerely hope you won't. The thought of having to interview prospective employees again fills me with horror after the parade of too-earnest applicants I've seen today.' Hal's lips shaped an ironic smile. 'Barring yourself, of course. If you're at all too earnest about having this job you hide it well. Would you like to see your room now?'

'Yes, I would.'

'Then follow me. In light of my accident, I thank God I chose an apartment that doesn't have stairs. For convenience, the room I've allocated you is next door to mine.' His hands resting lightly on the tyres of the wheelchair, Hal paused as another thought struck him.

'I won't give you a key because the revolving doors downstairs are never closed, and Charlie is usually there on the front desk if there's a problem. Plus, if you're out then that means I'm in, and all you need to do is get Charlie to buzz me to let me know you've returned. Okay?'

'But what if you've fallen asleep and don't hear the buzzer?'

'Unless I've been clubbed over the head by a particularly vindictive burglar you don't need to be concerned about that. I don't easily fall asleep—at least certainly not during the day. But, just to reassure you, Charlie has a spare key for emergencies.'

'That's good to know.'

'Then let's go and look at your room, shall we?'

CHAPTER TWO

IT HAD BEEN a hell of a day, Hal reflected, positioning his wheelchair in front of the bathroom mirror in order to brush his teeth. Although it was practically unheard of for him to turn in before midnight, since returning home from the hospital he'd cultivated the habit of retiring early in the hope of getting some longed-for rest. The irony was, no matter how early he went to bed, his sleep was unfailingly broken. First by episodes of agonising pain in his leg that meant he had to rise in order to take some pain relief and then by the inevitable visits to the bathroom—which was no easy feat when he had to hoist himself into his wheelchair to get there.

The one light on the horizon was he'd been advised that from tomorrow he could start using crutches. But he knew it would still be a fiasco, endeavouring to do all the commonplace things that he'd been used to taking for granted. Rubbing a hand round his dark stubbled jaw, then peering closer to examine the shocking bruised shadows beneath his eyes, he felt frustration and fury bite into him with all the force of a serrated steel clamp. *Was it usual to feel this fatigued after an accident? And was it normal that his emotions should be so tightly wound that he could scarcely contain them?*

His highly esteemed surgeon had assured him that it was…except the confirmation didn't help him to accept the fact. Thank God Sam had persuaded him to hire some practical help and companionship, with the aim of alleviating some of the frustration he felt round his compromised mobility and also to counter the boredom of being forced to spend so much time on his own.

If Sam hadn't been the manager of a busy psychology practice she would have willingly been there for Hal night and day if necessary. But she also had a husband with a demanding job, and Greg was surely entitled to spend his precious free time with his wife. As for Hal's so-called 'friends'…they were busy with their own demanding careers and pleasurable pursuits—and anyway none of them were the type to give up their time willingly for an invalid.

Appalled that he had begun to think of himself in such a scornful way, he quickly brushed his teeth, turned off the light, then returned to his bedroom grimly to face another disagreeable and painful night with nothing but his steadily worsening thoughts to keep him company.

As he lifted his hard-muscled frame out of the wheelchair and manoeuvred himself onto the bed he found himself fervently hoping that the feisty Kit Blessington's presence would at least be *bearable*. Perish the thought that she might be the type of woman who chattered incessantly about inconsequential things and would very quickly get on his nerves, making him bitterly regret hiring her—even if her practical skills *should* prove to be as competent as she'd indicated.

Hal was having an early-morning cup of coffee with his sister when, true to her word, Kit Blessington arrived at the agreed time. Sam had dropped in on her way to work, determined to meet Hal's new hired help as soon as possible, so she'd told him, her cat-like green eyes formidably serious. He knew it mattered to her a great deal that the woman passed muster because she adored her 'little' brother. He might resent her acting like his mother from time to time, but he didn't deny it felt good to have her unstinting regard and concern. Especially when the only communication he'd had from his father since the accident was a curt e-mail that had included the line, 'Didn't I always tell you that pride comes before a fall?'

Kick me while I'm down, why don't you? Hal had thought bitterly.

Tall and slender, with a gamine short hairstyle, his sister Sam looked as chic and sophisticated as always that morning in an elegant trouser suit. When Kit arrived the younger woman's bohemian, far more relaxed mode of dress couldn't have been more of a contrast. When he opened the door to let her in he saw that today her glorious red hair was precariously arranged up in a loose topknot that suggested it might easily topple at any moment, such must be the weight of the waving strands. Wearing a mint-green baggy knitted sweater beneath a man's battered tan flying jacket, along with a pair of slim-fitting caramel cords, she was transporting what looked to be a fairly hefty brown suitcase.

Hal immediately told her to put it down before she dislocated her shoulder, adding, 'What have you got in there? The kitchen sink?'

Flushing, she retorted, 'You *did* say that this was a live-in position? All I've brought with me are the strictest essentials, Mr Treverne.'

'Well, clearly they must indeed be essential if you're trying to lug *that* beast around,' he commented dryly.

Sam stepped up beside him and once Kit had sensibly lowered her suitcase down onto the parquet floor she leaned towards the younger woman to shake her hand.

'I'm very pleased to meet you, Ms Blessington. You've arrived just in the nick of time. Henry's got to get to grips with using his crutches today, so your presence will undoubtedly be appreciated. I'm Samantha Whyte, by the way—Henry's sister.'

'Hello. It's nice to meet you too, Ms Whyte. It's good to know that your brother has a close relative living nearby. It must be very reassuring for him in light of what he's coping with.'

'I don't live that near, but I'm close enough to call in whenever I can to check that he's okay. I have to warn you—Hal doesn't take to being confined very easily. Hal is what family and friends call him, by the way. He's apt to be like a bear with a sore head most days.'

'Do you two mind not talking about me as if I wasn't here?' Biting back an angry expletive, Hal violently reversed his wheelchair and headed back towards the kitchen.

'Don't mind him,' he heard Sam say soothingly behind him to Kit. 'As I said, he's a bit more irritable than usual since he broke his leg, but—'

'Don't you *dare* tell her that underneath my tetchy, disagreeable exterior I'm a veritable pussycat!' he yelled. 'Because I'm certainly *not!*'

His heart thumping hard inside his chest, Hal steered the wheelchair into the kitchen and straight away moved across to the oblong glass dining table to retrieve his rapidly cooling mug of coffee. He knew he was behaving like the worst bore in the world but he couldn't seem to help it. Tonight, before bed, he might just have to succumb to taking those sleeping pills his doctor had prescribed. Right now he'd probably take the strongest ones he could lay his hands on if they would help him get at least an hour of unbroken sleep. *'A bear with a sore head'* didn't come anywhere near to describing the infuriated way he felt.

'…and you'll need to consult with Hal's doctor today, when you take him to the hospital for his check-up, to get some advice on how best to help him.' Sam's voice carried clearly as she and Kit came down the hallway towards the kitchen. 'His knee joint and muscles were damaged when he broke his femur, and there's a certain process you have to know. Don't worry—it's not difficult. I think it's called the RICE technique, which stands for—'

'Rest, ice, compression and elevation,' Kit cut in quietly. 'I've been studying quite a comprehensive first-aid book since I was told that Mr Treverne had a broken femur. I've also spoken to one of my trainers at the centre where I took my first-aid courses.'

She'd been studying a first-aid book? Even though he was irritated at being discussed as though he were a recalcitrant schoolboy who'd complained about having to miss his school's sports day because he'd contracted chicken pox, Hal owned to feeling mildly surprised that his temporary employee would go to such lengths even before she knew if she had the job or not.

'I'm impressed.' Sam's voice contained the suggestion of a smile.

'Please don't be. My intention is simply to do a good job. It's no more than I would normally do when the person I've been hired to help is either recovering from an illness or an injury, Ms Whyte.'

'Please—call me Sam. At any rate, I've spoken to Hal's consultant about talking to you, so he's expecting you to ask.' They came into the kitchen. 'You can also check with the nurse who comes in once a week to visit him. Oh, and one more thing—there's also a cleaner who comes in twice a week to give the place a good going over. Mrs Baker is her name. So you won't have to spend too much time doing housework. My brother's welfare is your main priority. If he wants you to spend the entire day watching films or listening to music with him, then please don't hesitate.'

'Are you quite finished? Only I'm beginning to feel like some expendable extra in a hospital soap opera!' Scowling, Hal returned his mug of coffee to the table with a heavy slam, so that the now tepid beverage slopped over the lip and splashed onto his arm.

Without preamble, Kit moved across to the sink at lightning speed and grabbed the kitchen cloth that was folded over the tap. Then she hurried over to him, expertly dabbing the cloth on his exposed forearm and drying the spill. It was fortunate that he'd rolled up the sleeves of his cashmere sweater earlier, he thought wryly, because the blue was a favourite of his. But he guessed that, if required, his efficient new helper would no doubt have a handy solution for removing coffee stains from delicate fabrics too.

'Thanks,' he murmured when she had finished the clean-up.

'You're welcome.'

Her blue-eyed smile was fleeting, but with a jolt of surprise Hal straight away intuited that when she smiled properly—for instance when and if something pleased her—the gesture would light up her face and render her almost bewitching…

'Can I make you a fresh cup of coffee, Mr Treverne?' she asked.

Briefly catching his sister's amused glance over her shoulder, Hal shrugged. 'Yes—why not? I guess I'll be even more like a bear with a sore head if I don't have my usual quota of caffeine.'

'How do you take it?'

'Black with one sugar. You should make one for yourself too.'

'Thanks—I will. By the way, what time do you need to get to the hospital for your appointment?'

'Ten o'clock.'

'Of course. I remember that now.' The redhead gave him another fleeting smile. 'That gives us some time to have a general chat about things. For instance, you'll need to tell me what car I'm driving. Is it big enough to accommodate your wheelchair? Because if you're not used to using your crutches yet you're going to need it.'

Not wanting to contemplate the possibility of not being immediately expert at using crutches, Hal was terse. 'If it should transpire that I need the wheelchair—and I very much doubt it—then no doubt the hospital will supply one for my visit. The car you'll be driving me to my appointment in has plenty of leg room and is easy to drive…that is as long as you're a good driver?'

Again, if he'd thought to disconcert Kit then he was disappointed. With a confident toss of her head she moved over to the coffee machine and threw over her shoulder, 'I took my advanced driving test last year and passed with flying colours…so you can rest assured that I'm a good driver, Mr Treverne.'

'I thought we'd agreed you could call me Hal?'

'Do you mind if I call you Henry instead? Only using your friends' name for you sounds a little too over-familiar.'

Seeing the lightly mocking glint in his sister's eyes, Hal inwardly squirmed. No doubt his clever sister was thinking he'd met his match in the redoubtable Kit Blessington. But he would make it his mission to prove her wrong…see if he didn't!

'Well.' Sam leant down and dropped an affectionate peck on his cheek. 'I'll be off now. I'll leave you to the tender ministrations of Ms Blessington.' Her mouth curved into a satisfied and humorous grin.

'I'm not looking for her ministrations to be "tender",' he snapped. 'A decent level of competence will be enough.'

'A typical Hal response,' his sister remarked cheerily, winking at the other woman as she transported a mug of fresh coffee over to her brother. 'By the way, Kit, if you need me for anything…anything at all… you'll find my phone numbers on the noticeboard in Hal's study. You'll find that just to the side of a poster of the latest scantily clad supermodel. Look after him for me, won't you?'

'Of course.'

Unable to suppress a grin at his sister's amusing parting shot, Hal murmured, 'Bye, sis. Go easy with those wounded patients of yours, won't you?'

'What a lovely woman,' Kit remarked when Sam had departed.

'She is.' As he tunnelled his long fingers through hair

that hadn't seen a comb for more days than he cared to mention, Hal's smile was unrestrained. 'I agree. She's certainly one in a million.'

Momentarily dazzled by the twinkling hazel eyes and curved masculine mouth before her, Kit shrugged off her heavy jacket and arranged it on the back of one of the shaker-style dining chairs positioned around the table. Then she curled a stray strand of copper hair round her ear and in a brisk but friendly tone asked, 'Shall I help you get to grips with your walking aids now? We've got some spare time for you to practise before we leave for the hospital.'

Even though his smile had all but made her catch her breath she hadn't missed the fact that her employer's skin looked almost grey with tiredness, and her heart couldn't help but go out to him. More importantly, she reminded herself, she was there to do a job and help ease his burden and she was anxious to make a start.

'Wouldn't you like to take your luggage to your room first and unpack?'

Touched by his unexpected thoughtfulness, Kit shook her head.

'I can do that later. I'd rather help you first.'

Underneath what she guessed was a complexion that was far paler than usual, Hal flushed visibly.

'Crutches it is, then. You *do* realise you're going to have to let me lean on you a little while I get my balance?'

'That won't be a problem. I assure you that I'm much stronger than I look.'

'Why did I know you'd say that?'

For a second time Henry Treverne's devastating smile came very close to turning Kit's knees to water.

She fervently reminded herself to be on her guard round that killer smile. It would be extremely foolish to trust it. Once before she'd been beguiled by the smile of a handsome man and against her better judgement, had fallen into a brief affair with him. When the man in question had turned out to be married, Kit had been devastated. Not just because he had lied to her about being free, but because it had struck at the very core of her ability to trust herself. *There'd been no excuse.* After seeing what her mother had gone through with mendacious faithless men she ought to have known better. One thing was certain: she wouldn't make the same mistake twice…

Assuming the best 'head girl' tone she could muster, she said firmly to Hal, 'Well, I suppose we'd better get on with it, then.'

There was no disputing her new employer's indomitable spirit, Kit mused as, with her help, Henry carefully lowered himself onto a comfortable padded seat in the plush waiting room. But neither had it been hard to detect his frustration at not being able to master the use of his walking aids as smoothly and as effortlessly as he might have wished. Once again the sweat that had broken out on his brow had illustrated the effort it had taken him to get this far. They'd only walked the short distance from the car park, but it had clearly been a struggle for Hal. It made her even more determined to help him achieve the goal of being confident with the aids.

Leaning towards him, Kit freed his hands from holding the crutches and carefully leaned them against the wall behind him.

'You'd better go and tell the receptionist that I'm here.'

The sudden command sounded like a snarl of anger and resentment—a bit like a wounded animal. But she wasn't about to take Hal's surly mood personally. In her time working for the agency she'd encountered several 'tricky' customers and had soon learned how best to handle them. People were dealing with all kinds of challenges. Not just physical and mental ones, but also more commonplace dilemmas, like bereavement and loneliness and sometimes the heartache caused by a failed relationship.

Even though her mother had tested her patience to the nth degree, Kit was a naturally compassionate person, and it helped her more easily cope with the frayed tempers and impatience of some of the clients she cared for and not let their volatile reactions undermine her.

'Okay, I'll go and get you booked in. Do you have a patient card or a letter with your hospital number on?'

Hal sucked in a breath and blew it out again, as if even more exasperated. His eyes glinted, warning her that his temper was hanging by the slimmest of threads.

'Why? Do you think they don't know who I am?' he snapped.

Mentally taking a deep breath of her own, Kit said calmly, 'I'm sure the Queen herself has a patient number, and everybody knows who *she* is.'

'Never mind the backchat, Ms Blessington. Just go and tell them I'm here, will you?'

Had she imagined it or had that handsome carved mouth of his twitched ever so slightly with amusement? Acutely aware of the pretty young receptionist, who was gazing across the room at Hal as though he were some sublime visitation from heaven, Kit went to the desk.

'I'm here with Mr Henry Treverne. He has a ten o'clock appointment with his consultant Mr Shadik.'

Reluctantly withdrawing her gaze from Hal, the girl answered, 'I'll let him know that Mr Treverne is here right away.'

'Thank you.'

Returning to sit beside her brooding charge, Kit proffered what she hoped was a reassuring smile. 'Hopefully you won't have too long to wait.'

His dark eyebrows beetling together, Hal growled, 'However long the wait, it's far too long for my liking.'

'Don't you want help to get better?'

When he turned his head towards her she was treated to the full force of his powerful gaze.

'You may have noticed that asking for help and accepting it is not something that comes naturally to me.'

'Then perhaps when you're back to full strength again it might be something you could start to cultivate?'

'Yeah—and my father might train to climb Mount Everest!'

'I take it he's not a keen climber like you are, then?'

'The only thing he climbs are walls—especially when he hears of another "foolhardy escapade" of mine that he despairs of. That's why he didn't visit me in the hospital when I had this blasted accident. He's a man who's always erred on the side of safety. The only risks he ever takes are ones that he's sure will preserve the legacy of Falteringham House for the generations of the Treverne family to come.'

'Falteringham House? Is that the name of your family home?'

'Yes.'

'And your father really didn't visit you when you broke your leg?' *No wonder he was acting like some kind of wounded animal. It had clearly hurt him that his father had stayed away when he'd been injured.* She doubted that even her impractical, flighty mother would have behaved as callously.

Hal's expression was far away for a moment, and seconds later a tall, elegant man dressed in a tailored pinstriped suit that suggested he might just as easily be a wealthy lawyer as a surgeon presented himself in front of the man sitting beside her.

'Mr Treverne. It is good to see you again. Would you like to come into the examination room and I'll take a look at that leg, see how things are progressing?'

The comment was impatiently received with a disdainfully curled lip. 'The only thing that's progressed is the pain, Mr Shadik.'

'Then perhaps I need to prescribe some stronger medication for you. Let us go and discuss it, shall we?'

Glancing round at Kit, Hal nodded towards the crutches she'd leant against the wall.

'Give me a hand with those, would you? And you may as well come into the examination room with me and get the gist of what's happening.'

'I think that's a good idea.' Immediately pushing to her feet, Kit helped him safely secure the armrests before assisting him to stand. When he did, she observed that once again his indomitably handsome brow was beaded with sweat. The consultant had also noted it, and gravely shook his head.

'I am certain we can do much better as far as your pain relief is concerned, Henry, so please don't worry. Today is your first day on crutches, is it not?'

Hal briefly dipped his head in agreement.

'We'll get another X-ray and afterwards you can see the physio to make sure that you're using the aids properly... But I can see that you're already a natural.' The surgeon beamed.

Kit sensed that beneath his grim smile Henry was privately utilising every expletive he could lay his hands on, as well as inventing a few more choice ones of his own...

CHAPTER THREE

HAL HAD BEEN in dire need of a rest when they'd returned from the hospital. After the tedious rounds of X-rays and physiotherapy he'd endured, as well as a further consultation about the results with his surgeon, he'd been so exhausted that the only thing he'd longed for was at least a couple of hours of unbroken sleep.

In the living room he'd allowed Kit to assist him in getting comfortable on the couch, privately surprised at how used to her touch he was getting and how quickly he had started to trust it.

The biggest surprise of all had come when he'd learned what an amazingly confident driver she was. His top-of-the-range sporty four-by-four had been handled as expertly as if Hal was driving it himself. Any fears about her denting or damaging one of his favourite cars were happily unfounded.

But when Kit had been gently about to drape a cashmere throw over him as he lay back against the couch cushions he'd instantly reverted to type and snapped, 'For God's sake, woman! Stop fussing, will you?'

After that he'd despatched her to her room to unpack and acclimatise herself to her new surroundings, telling her to leave him in peace for a while. When she'd shut the door behind her, as he'd instructed, he'd closed his eyes only to find that the scent of her floral perfume lingered a little too disturbingly for his peace of mind. To compound the disturbance he'd also recalled just then how her precariously arranged topknot had finally collapsed during his consultation, spilling over her shoulders in a vivid autumnal riot of auburn silk. After that it had taken Hal quite a bit longer than he'd hoped to finally slip into the deep slumber he'd craved…

When he awoke it was to a darkened room, with thundering rain pouring outside. The downpour was so fierce that it lashed against the window panes as if trying to force an entry. It must be quite some storm for it to be so dark this early. Manoeuvring himself upright, he roughly scrubbed the backs of his knuckles across his eyelids and yawned. The sudden realisation that he was in dire need of the bathroom made him immediately seek out his walking aids. When he saw that they had been leant against an armchair a few feet away he muttered a ripe curse beneath his breath. How the *hell* was he supposed to reach them over there? The uncharacteristic sense of helplessness that swept over him made him feel even more irritated.

'Kit!' he yelled. 'Where the hell are you? I need you in here *now*!'

The door opened almost straight away and variously placed lamps flooded the room with softly diffused lighting. The first thing Hal noticed was that his new assistant had tamed her riot of auburn hair back into its precarious topknot. He didn't rightly know why that should be such a crime, but to his thinking it *was*.

'I need my crutches,' he said gruffly, carefully

swinging his legs to the floor. 'I'm pretty desperate to get to the bathroom.'

Without a word she immediately went across to the armchair to collect them, then returned to stand in front of him.

'It might be quicker if you lean on me and hop. It's just a few feet away, isn't it?'

'Sweetheart.' He glanced up into her pretty blue eyes and intoned, gravel-voiced, 'I'm six-foot-two and no lightweight. I have only your word that you're stronger than you look, and I'd rather not risk you getting a broken leg to match mine. Just help me with the crutches, will you?'

A little more *au fait* with the walking aids since his session with the physiotherapist, Hal was nonetheless pleased to see that Kit had waited for him when he emerged from the bathroom. Keeping a close eye on him, she silently accompanied him back down the hallway and into the living room.

'Would you like me to get on with dinner now?' she asked.

Dropping down onto the couch, he stared blankly out of the window, suddenly hypnotised by the still hammering rain. 'It looks pretty bleak out there, doesn't it?' he commented.

'Perhaps it's not so bad being forced to stay in this evening in light of the weather?'

There it was again...that surprisingly engaging smile. It completely transformed her otherwise serious demeanour and made Hal think she should smile more often. Not wanting to linger on the idea, he found himself nodding in agreement. For someone who prided himself on not letting even the most extreme weather conditions prevent him from doing what he wanted if he could help it, it was probably a first. Then it struck him what Kit had said just before that last remark.

His brows drawing together in puzzlement, he asked, 'Shouldn't we be having lunch first?'

'I'm afraid lunchtime has come and gone, Mr Treverne. You've been asleep since we got back from the hospital and that was nearly four hours ago. It's just after six in the evening.'

He was genuinely shocked. 'You're joking?'

The slender shoulders beneath the mint-green sweater lifted in a gently amused shrug. 'I promise you I'm not.'

'Did I take a sleeping pill before I napped? I don't remember...'

'No, you didn't. I think sheer exhaustion probably made you sleep so well. Anyway, you must be hungry. I saw that the fridge was well stocked and I took the liberty of making a beef bolognaise while you were sleeping. By the way, I checked with the agency that you weren't a vegetarian. I've just got to rustle up some pasta and I'll bring it in to you.'

'Sounds good. But I'll only eat it if you push me in my chair into the dining room and then come and join me. I really can't abide eating my meals off of a tray, and neither can I abide eating alone. I feel decrepit enough as it is in my sorry state, without acting like an invalid.'

Kit's expression was visibly perturbed. 'That sounds as though you believe you don't deserve any acknowledgement of your condition at all. Isn't that why you hired me in the first place, Mr Treverne? Because you needed some help?'

'How many times do I have to tell you to stop calling me Mr Treverne? And for pity's sake please don't keep referring to me as needing help. It's becoming the bane of my life.'

It wasn't her reference to his need that was bothering him, Kit guessed. It was the fact that for probably the first time ever this fit, active and no doubt fiercely independent businessman and sportsman *had* to be dependent on others…a state he undoubtedly despised. In truth, she entirely sympathised. She would hate it too.

'Well, I'll just go into the kitchen and cook the pasta, then I'll come back and take you into the dining room.'

Stretching out his hand for the mobile phone he'd left on the coffee table, Hal turned towards her.

'Take your time. I've got a couple of calls I want to make to my office first.'

'Okay. If you need me for anything, just call out.'

While Henry had been having his rest earlier Kit had made good use of the time to unpack, arrange her clothes in the walk-in wardrobe and arrange her toiletries in the bathroom. Despite there being an array of wonderfully scented products lined up on the shelves, she wouldn't be making use of them. After all, she was here to work, not as a guest. But she was more than appreciative of the beautiful room she'd been allocated. It had a lovely view of the large neatly mown communal gardens downstairs. The verdant green was bordered by a plethora of trees, plants and shrubs, and a person might almost fool herself that she was deep in the heart of the countryside instead of practically in the centre of London.

She'd also noticed the indisputably feminine touch that the room's decor suggested—such as the luxurious lilac curtains with matching swags that hung at the windows and the array of colourful cushions that were attractively arranged at the head of the Queen-sized bed. The silk pillows were made up of various vintage designs full of natural motifs like birds and flowers. *It was definitely not a man's room*. In fact the decor was the polar opposite of the very masculine chrome and glass furnishings that the apartment's owner obviously favoured. Was Hal's sister Sam's the female influence that had helped design it?

Dropping strands of linguine into a pan of boiling water in the kitchen, Kit pushed back her hair and frowned. *There'd been no mention of a girlfriend or fiancée*. If Henry Treverne had either then surely she would have been told of her existence in case the woman dropped in or telephoned? In the newspaper reports she'd read about the accident at the time there'd been no mention of a girlfriend—which, considering his 'playboy' reputation, had surprised her. Telling herself he must be between relationships, she dropped her shoulders and made herself relax. The job she did could be testing enough without relatives or 'significant others' keeping too close an eye on her. She always worked best when her clients trusted her judgement enough to know that she could be completely relied upon to take good care of her charge.

In the dining room that also shared a view of the communal gardens, Hal took four or five mouthfuls of the fragrant pasta Kit had carefully prepared and across the magnificent glass table gave her a rueful smile.

'This is really good,' he commented. 'But I can't say the same is true of my appetite since the accident. I'm afraid I'm going to have to leave it there. This must be a first. Anyone who knows me well would tell you that it's unheard of for me to leave anything. Usually I can eat for England.'

'Trauma can affect people in many different ways,' Kit answered thoughtfully. 'As I'm sure your sister must have told you.'

'Trust me…she *has*. Sometimes I wish she wasn't quite so *all knowing*.'

Wanting to convey her reassurance, and sensing that underneath the dry wit he was probably feeling understandably low, she didn't hesitate to smile. 'You shouldn't worry about not having much of an appetite. I'm sure it will return in a few days, when you've started to feel more comfortable about getting round on your crutches and are getting more sleep. Rest is one of the greatest healers, but in our fast-paced culture it's too often overlooked.'

Hal's golden eyes narrowed interestedly. 'You sound as if you have some strong views on the subject?'

Laying her fork and spoon down on her plate, Kit took a few moments to mull over the remark. 'Moving so fast puts a lot of strain and pressure on the body as well as on the mind.' She sighed. 'Sometimes we need to remind ourselves that we aren't machines. We're flesh and blood and bone, and an overload of stress and pressure can tip us over the edge as well as cause accidents.'

'Then I take it you definitely wouldn't approve of someone who regularly pushes their body to the max in the pursuit of being the best he can in any sport or activity he participates in?'

'I presume you're talking about yourself?' Her gaze met his arresting hazel eyes and she saw his pupils flare teasingly.

MAGGIE COX   45

'Yes, I am,' he confirmed, smiling. 'I put my heart and soul into everything I do…and I mean *everything*.'

Kit's body tightened at his emphasis and a distinct buzz of sensual heat sizzled through her. The strong reaction took her aback and caused her to feel unsettled for a moment. Willing back her composure—because in all likelihood it was second nature for a man like Hal to tease women and get them flustered—she reached for her fork with a matter-of-fact air and curled some linguine round it. The man was on a hiding to nothing if he thought to unhinge her with sexual innuendos to inflate his ego, she thought. *He'd soon come to learn that she was immune.*

'I'm sure that's commendable,' she commented, 'but it can also be dangerous when a desire to be competitive becomes the driving force in everything you do. Wasn't that how you came to have your accident in the first place?'

The teasing smile completely vanished from her companion's handsome face. 'I suppose you read that in the newspapers?' Plucking his linen napkin from where he'd laid it across his lap, Hal threw it down on the table in disgust and scowled. 'Newspaper reporters aren't exactly known for telling the truth, you know.'

'Was that a fabrication, then? That you were racing a business rival on a ski slope that's considered to be one of the most extreme terrains in the mountains?'

'You know what, Kit Blessington? If you ever think about a change of career you ought to consider becoming a public prosecutor. You certainly don't take any prisoners.'

Directly meeting his irritated glance, Kit shrugged. 'That's where you're wrong. I would hate to be responsible for condemning anyone…whether I was paid to do it or not. And although I don't think of what I do as a career, exactly, I'm quite happy earning my living at it and endeavouring to deliver a good service.'

Hearing the heavy sigh Hal emitted following her statement, she thought she'd better rein in her propensity to call a spade a spade before she talked herself out of a job. Antagonising a man who was already struggling to come to terms with an injury that severely restricted his usual activities was really not a good idea.

'I'm sorry if I've offended you with my opinions,' she said quickly. 'I have no desire to upset you. I suppose I just get a little passionate about the things that I believe are right.'

'Everyone is entitled to their views, and being passionate isn't a crime.'

There was the briefest suggestion of a smile on his beautifully carved lips and Kit was reassured.

'In my book being passionate just means that you care,' Henry continued, 'Which is why I take the risks I do in my work and in the sports that I love. And besides, it's in the male DNA to be competitive…survival of the fittest and all that.'

Unable to curb the impulse, she leaned towards him. 'I hear what you're saying, but don't you get tired of having to conform to that ethos all the time?'

Rolling his eyes, Hal grimaced. 'Right now I don't exactly have much choice, do I?'

'I tell you what…' Rising to her feet, Kit had a sudden brainwave. 'Why don't I make us a pot of coffee and I'll cut you a slice of home-made fruitcake to go with it? I know you didn't feel much like eating your dinner, but that could be dessert.'

'We've got home-made fruitcake?' His previously glum expression was transformed by the most beguiling boyish grin she had ever seen.

Crossing her arms over her mint-green sweater, she couldn't help smiling back. 'I brought it with me from home. I made it last night. When I rang the agency to confirm that I'd got the job the manager told me that it was one of your favourites.'

'Sam probably tipped her off. She knows I've a real weakness for cake…particularly fruitcake.'

'Well, then, why don't you just sit and relax and I'll go and get you some?'

'Don't forget the coffee.'

'I won't.'

As Hal lingered over his coffee Kit disappeared into the kitchen to stack the dishwasher. With a contented sigh he stretched out his long legs on the couch and winced as familiar intermittent pain shot down his calf. For once he didn't allow it to destroy his equilibrium. In truth, he regretted not making a better effort with the aromatic pasta Kit had cooked, but he'd immensely enjoyed the fruitcake she'd made. It was probably one of the best cakes he'd ever eaten. One thing was certain: if that was an example of her attention to detail on behalf of the people she worked for then she couldn't be faulted.

Utilising the remote device by his side, Hal turned up the volume on the soothing music he was listening to. If he could just learn to curtail the impatience and restlessness that had plagued him since the accident had immobilised him then perhaps he could start to enjoy the enforced rest that he was faced with? It had literally been *years* since he'd had some proper respite. Most days he lived his life as though he were in a race to get to the finish line first.

In a bid to divert the less than comfortable realisation, he returned his thoughts to Kit. There was something about the feisty redhead's presence that was undeniably reassuring. What had helped her become so capable and pragmatic? *He was curious to know.* Maybe over the next few days he would try to draw her out and get to know her a little? The women in his life had always bemoaned the fact that Hal didn't give them enough of his time and attention—be they the girlfriends he'd had or his sister Sam—because he was inevitably obsessed with work and also the high-octane sports activities he favoured. If he made it a bit of a project to find out more about Kit's background by conversing with her and really listening to what she had to say then it might help him learn how to improve his relationships with women in the future. *At any rate, it was worth a try.* Seeing as though all his usual distractions were denied him because of his injury, why not just embrace what was available instead?

Another knifing pain shot through his leg, but it was mostly concentrated on the muscles in his knee that had been damaged. Just as he reached down to massage it the door opened and Kit returned. As if intuiting he was in some discomfort, she came straight over to him with a concerned frown.

'I think I should get you some ice for that knee. But first let me put some pillows underneath you to elevate it. If we do that every day then it will help reduce the swelling.'

'You're the boss,' Hal quipped ruefully.

'It's good to know you don't have a problem with a woman being in charge.'

'This is a one time and one time only deal. My tolerance and acceptance will only stretch so far. Once I'm back on my feet again you'd be unwise to push any advantage you'd gained while I was laid up.'

Raising her brows, Kit responded smartly, 'When you're back on your feet again you'll no longer need my services, so such a possibility won't even arise. I'll be looking after another client…hopefully one a little less egotistical than you. Now, I'll just go and get a couple of pillows to elevate that knee.'

Any response he might normally have made to such an unflattering observation worryingly deserted Hal. The idea that Kit was already eagerly contemplating a new client—one 'a little less egotistical' than he was—seriously bothered him. And neither did he welcome the sense of vulnerability it left him with. Weakness of any kind didn't sit well with him.

As she exited the room to fetch the pillows he breathed out a disgruntled sigh. But when she returned carrying them, and leaned towards him to carry out the necessary manoeuvre, he immediately noted that her smooth alabaster cheeks had a faintly scarlet tint to them. *How interesting,* he thought. Perhaps it wasn't just his egotistical nature that ruffled this coolly efficient redhead?

'Lift up,' she instructed, her bright blue eyes skimming his features with the merest brief glance.

Raising himself in order that she could slide the pillows beneath him, Hal wasn't about to let the fact go unremarked…

'You're blushing, Ms Blessington. Does it disturb

you to get this close to your client? Because if it does I don't know how you're going to manage when you help me into my bath later,' he taunted.

Carefully assisting him to lower his legs down onto the pillows, Kit met his amused glance with a similarly mocking one.

'If you think it's going to make me squirm with embarrassment seeing an injured man in his birthday suit then I hate to disappoint you, *Mr Treverne*. Trust me— I've seen it all before!'

For the second time in a few short minutes Hal found himself worryingly bereft of an apt rejoinder and he didn't like it. He didn't like it *one* bit!

CHAPTER FOUR

THE LUXURIOUS BATHROOM adjacent to Hal's equally opulent bedroom had a vast sunken bath and shower and a gleaming marble floor with a striking snakeskin finish. If Kit hadn't known it to be true already, it screamed out that its owner was undoubtedly male, seriously charismatic and frighteningly rich. And so far her new employer was proving to be the most challenging one she'd ever worked for...

Dropping down onto a seriously comfy-looking chair, Hal handed over his crutches to her without preamble. It was nearly eleven o'clock at night and Kit knew that he was still tired, still hurting, and cranky because of it. Trying not to pay too much attention to the unhappy expression on his handsome face, she stood the crutches against the wall, leant down to the bath and turned on the taps.

As the water gushed out into the tub she glanced over her shoulder and asked, 'What kind of temperature do you like?'

'What?'

He was staring at her as though in a trance. Straightening, she crossed her arms over her chest, feeling as though she were suddenly being examined under the searching glare of an intense spotlight. It was hard to string a single coherent thought together when her heart felt as though she was careening downhill at breakneck speed because it beat so fast.

'I asked what kind of temperature you wanted?'

'Hot.'

Such a simple, commonplace word shouldn't sound so…so *provocative*. But it *did*. And it didn't help her case that she remembered telling Hal that she was hardly fazed by seeing a man's naked body and had 'seen it all before'. She didn't doubt he thought she must be referring to her intimate experiences. Perhaps he thought she'd had several? The truth was she'd had just one briefly intimate liaison and that had turned out to be an unmitigated *disaster*. She'd been stupidly bluffing when she'd made her comment, so that he wouldn't think he had the upper hand. And she'd called *him* egotistical!

'Okay,' she said.

'I'll need you to help me get in the water—also to put the waterproof cast protector on.'

'Of course.'

'Then I suppose I'd better get undressed.'

Swallowing hard at the very idea of seeing this man's toned, athletic body bared for her eyes only—albeit so that he could take a bath—Kit had to dig deep to retain her composure. 'Do you need any assistance with that?' she asked.

Hal's golden eyes glimmered almost painfully.

'Not to get undressed, no. But you might as well stay in here until I'm ready to get into the bath. Think you can do that?'

'No problem.' She sensed heat flare in her cheeks even before she answered.

'I'll put a towel round me to spare your blushes,' he declared, his tone indisputably provocative. 'Even though you've assured me that you've seen it all before.'

Kit might have known he wouldn't let her forget she'd said that. 'Do you want me to put in some bath salts or foam?' she enquired.

'Some of that blue stuff on the shelf will do,' he responded blithely, as if it scarcely mattered.

The 'blue stuff' he'd indicated was a seriously high-end exclusive product that probably cost the earth, she noted, a helpless little smile curving her lips. It certainly smelt nice. While Hal lifted off his sweater and T-shirt she kept herself occupied by watching over the bath-water and regularly testing the temperature. When he indicated that he was ready she turned off the taps and swivelled to see that he had wound a slim white bath-towel round the lower half of his torso, while he supported his injured leg on a handy footstool.

But that wasn't the only thing Kit noticed. Exposed in all their glory, the sheer tantalising breadth of his shoulders and his strongly defined biceps were even more magnificent than she'd guessed they would be. But she couldn't afford to let the fact distract her...not even for a second.

'The bath is ready, so I think we'd better get the cast protector on,' she said briskly.

'Then let's do it.'

With the waterproof protector fitted over his cast, Kit made sure to support him strongly as Hal gingerly lowered himself into the fragrant bubbles. Her heart raced in concern when she felt his muscles tensing and saw him bite his lip. 'Is the water too hot?' she breathed.

As she assisted him to position his injured leg on one of the marble bath sides he surprised her with an unrestrained grin. 'It's perfect. Just the way I like it.'

'Good...that's good.'

His even white teeth flashed another smile as he reached down beneath the bubbles to produce the now sopping wet towel that he'd wound round his hips to spare Kit's blushes. He handed it to her.

'You have no idea *how* good.'

Carrying the wet towel over to one of the pair of marble sinks to wring it out, she almost had to bite back a groan. She'd never known that just the sound of a man's voice could be such a turn-on. And it didn't help her to stay as safely immune as she wanted to when the man was as physically imposing and arresting as Hal Treverne.

She was appalled at herself for even daring to fantasise about someone like him when he had a reputation for dating some of the most beautiful women in the world. She didn't delude herself that she came anywhere *near* that elite category! She reminded herself of the cast-iron rules she always worked by—to be utterly professional and impartial at all times and definitely not to get personally involved. Particularly when the client was a stunningly attractive male who wasn't averse to teasing and provoking her. The last thing she wanted to do was find herself repeating the same soul-destroying pattern as her mother had...falling for a man who could only spell disaster. She'd already been burned by the brief, ill-judged liaison she'd had with a man who had turned out to be married...

'Kit?'

'Yes?' She finished wringing out the wet towel and turned her head to acknowledge him. The steam from the hot water had created a pall of fine damp mist over his sculpted cheekbones and had made his thick dark hair curl against his neck even more rebelliously. Aside from the fact that the mere sight of him challenged her on almost every level, Kit couldn't deny the pleasure she felt because he appeared so much more relaxed than she'd witnessed seeing him before.

'Will you wash my hair for me?'

It seemed she was going to have another challenge.

Helplessly, Kit swirled her tongue over her lips, because they'd suddenly dried. Leaving the damp towel coiled in the sink, she caught a glimpse of her own flushed face and startled blue eyes in the mirror. Her fiery copper hair was once again drifting free from its topknot and the bathroom steam had misted her porcelain skin to make her resemble a girl who had just got out of her lover's bed. Her insides executed a nervous cartwheel at the thought. *Particularly as the lover she'd automatically envisaged had been Hal...*

Smoothing her moist palms down over her jeans to dry them, Kit stepped slowly towards him. He was resting his head against the marble rim of the bath and she willed him not to notice how flushed she was. She desperately needed some time to restore her equilibrium. *For goodness' sake, he's injured,* she reminded herself. *I'm here to do a job and to help aid his recuperation by providing practical help...not to act like some silly infatuated schoolgirl around him!* She'd never been able to understand grown women who acted that way. And neither would she jeopardise her job or her peace of mind by mimicking them.

'Yes,' she replied. 'Of course I'll wash your hair. Do you have any preference as to what shampoo I should use?' It hadn't escaped her attention how laden with men's grooming products his bathroom shelves were, but once again he shrugged his shoulders as if the choice hardly signified.

'I don't have a preference. All I want is for you to wash my hair and help me feel halfway human again.'

'Okay. I'll just nip into the kitchen and get a jug so I can rinse the shampoo off. Won't be a minute.'

In the kitchen Kit found a suitable jug and gulped down a glass of cool water to help steady her nerves before returning to the steamy bathroom and the prospect of washing Hal Treverne's luxuriant dark hair...

Without a doubt Kit Blessington had a *sinful* touch, Hal reflected as her long graceful fingers massaged his scalp. It made him long for her to massage the rest of his battered and bruised body As well as giving him his broken femur and damaged knee, the accident hadn't spared him all the other aches and pains commensurate with a heavy fall.

Remembering the sight of her bending over the bath to run the water earlier, he noted that her fitted corduroy jeans couldn't help but emphasise her surprisingly lush curves. She had a derrière that resembled the most perfectly ripe peach. How could a healthy male specimen *not* fantasise about kissing it and perhaps taking a little nibble? It was only natural that his red-blooded imagination should start to linger irresistibly on the idea of making love to her. After all, he was only human, and having not had a woman in his bed for at least six months because of his killing work schedule and extra-curricular sporting pursuits he found his healthy libido was seriously starting to protest at the sexual drought he'd imposed on it. *Just because he had a broken leg it didn't mean that his need and desire for sex was broken too.*

Yet it didn't sit well with Hal that the sudden heated attraction he seemed to have developed towards Kit might compromise her in any way. Somehow he intuited that she wasn't a woman to take a sexual fling lightly…particularly not one with a man who had hired her to help him as he recuperated from an accident. So, no matter how tempting the alluring redhead was, he should leave well alone…for *both* their sakes, he decided.

Instead, he would carry out the intention he'd had earlier, to get to know her a little and engage her in conversation. He would encourage her to tell him a bit about *her* life rather than just talk about himself. God knew there was enough about his career and sporting exploits in the tabloids and magazines if she had a mind to read them… And it didn't stop there. There were plenty of unwelcome salacious reports about him too… Past associations with models and actresses, for instance, were embellished and exaggerated to the hilt. For some reason the thought of Kit reading about those made him wince…

'I'll rinse off the shampoo now,' she announced cheerfully. 'Then I'll get you some warm towels to dry yourself with. You can put your bathrobe on in the meantime.'

'Thanks, but just before you dash off there's something I have to do.' Spying a tiny bubble of foam on the tip of Kit's nose, where she had unthinkingly wiped the back of her hand across her face after washing his hair, Hal couldn't help staring.

'What's that?' she wanted to know. Her lips curved in an unknowingly sweet smile.

Unable to resist, he ordered huskily, 'Come here.'

'Why? What for?'

But even as she asked the question Kit was bending down towards him, to bring her face nearer to his, and the air between them thrummed with the kind of internal turbulence that was usually felt just before a lightning strike. Even though he might be dicing with danger, Hal couldn't ignore the irresistible impulse that had been building up inside him ever since she had helped him into the bath.

'You've got some foam on your nose,' he breathed, gently obliterating the tiny soap bubble with the pad of his thumb.

As soon as he'd seen to that he curved his hand round the back of her neck and brought her face down even closer to his. Her surprised breath fanned him softly just before he helplessly touched his mouth to hers for the briefest of seconds. He'd been longing to experience the taste of her, and it was a Herculean task not to surrender completely to the idea of kissing her more passionately, because everything about Kit Blessington had started to arouse him, Hal realised. Perhaps even more than it should, because in truth she should be strictly out of bounds to him.

Their association was nothing more than a professional one. She was the woman he'd hired as a home help. *But, oh, her cherry lips were sweet…*

Reluctantly he came to his senses and hastily withdrew. But he couldn't so easily escape the desire that burned in him as brightly and hotly as a flame that would not go out...

'You—we—we shouldn't have done that!' With her cheeks flushed and her eyes bright Kit self-consciously smoothed her hand down over her hip and reached for the jug of clean water she'd left on the bath side. 'I'd better rinse off your hair and then get those warm bath-towels for you.'

After rinsing the shampoo from his hair Kit grimly adhered to her task of helping Hal get out of the bath. She was careful not to meet his eyes so he wouldn't see that she was desperately struggling to maintain her composure. There was no hiding the fact that his naked physical form had deluged her with an uncomfortably primal awareness. That brief but inflammatory kiss he'd delivered had effectively turned her previously 'safe' little world upside down, and she didn't know how she was going to right it again.

Silently helping him into his bathrobe, Kit couldn't disguise her need to escape for a while. 'Will you be okay for a couple of minutes while I fetch those towels?'

'Of course. But don't be gone too long, will you? I might start to think you're trying to pretend that chaste little kiss we just shared didn't happen.'

Forcing herself to meet the undoubtedly mocking glance on Hal's face, she lifted her chin and delivered a deliberately droll reply of her own.

'I hate to dent your ego—I really do—but I've already forgotten about it. My focus is entirely on your welfare, just as it should be. When I return, I'll stay and help you dress, if you'd like? I'm aware you've already expended quite a bit of energy today, and you need to rest that leg.'

Hal predictably scowled. 'I don't need help dressing. Just bring me the towels. After that, rather than have you stay and help me, I'd prefer it if you just went and made me a hot drink.'

'Your wish is my command.'

'I wouldn't push your luck if I were you.'

'I wouldn't dare,' Kit murmured softly, and quickly exited the room…

She came back soon afterwards with the promised towels, then disappeared again to make his drink. Hal couldn't help feeling a little sombre. He'd told her that rather than staying to help him he'd prefer her to go and make him a hot drink, but it was a *lie*. He didn't prefer that she'd done that at all. His assertion that he didn't want her help because he hated being so reliant on her, and also because everything about her was arousing him…almost to the point of *pain*.

Hefting a heavy sigh, he glared down at his inanimate broken limb with a feeling that was very close to despair. Being left with too much time on his hands in which to berate himself for creating such a horrendous situation was hardly helpful. *He hated being left alone with his thoughts*. He'd rather go sky-diving or climb a glacial mountain without a guide rope any day. At least when he was doing that there wasn't any time for painful brooding—not when his attention had to be absolutely focused on the exhilarating and dangerous task in hand if he wanted to stay alive.

Breaking his leg and being forced to take time out from his usual activities had made Hal realise just how alone and fearful of the future he'd become lately. Having woken up to the fact that he'd deluded himself for too long that money, a successful career and the extreme sports he favoured were enough to keep his loneliness and sense of emptiness at bay, he was now faced with the realisation that in truth he'd been hiding from the one thing that might help counteract that…*having a genuinely intimate and meaningful relationship with a woman.* He'd avoided the possibility like the plague thus far, due to his dread fear of commitment. *In any case, he was hardly a good bet.* Aside from his restless nature, he was far too selfish and self-obsessed, and sooner or later the woman he chose would discover that and leave…*just as his mother had left his father when Hal and Sam were small…*

Uncomfortably ill at ease with that particular train of thought, he stood up abruptly on his good leg and reached out a hand for one of the crutches Kit had left standing against the wall close to his chair. Intent on positioning the padded rest under his arm, he lost his balance. Shockingly, he pitched forward onto the marble floor. Grunting out a furious expletive, because the force of the fall had momentarily robbed him of his breath, he stayed there for several humiliating seconds before coming to his senses and shouting for Kit.

He heard her run down the parquet corridor and for a moment couldn't help envying her ability to do just that—to run freely without hindrance…

'What on earth happened?'

Dropping to her haunches beside him in concern, she laid a hand gently on his back. Hal swore he could feel the warmth of her soft skin radiate through the thick towelling robe he wore.

Turning his head towards her, he grimaced. 'What

do you think happened? That I suddenly had a sudden perverse yen to lie face-down on the marble?'

Ignoring his mocking retort, Kit suddenly saw the walking aid lying on the floor beside him and realised what had happened.

'No, but I think you must have had a perverse yen to play Superman. No one is infallible, Henry…not even you. Why didn't you call me to come and help you stand up? That's what I'm here for. Are you hurt?'

'You mean apart from my pride? No. I don't think so. Help me get to my feet, then I can check.'

Upright again, and leaning on her with his hard-muscled arm draped round her shoulders, Kit guided him back to the bathroom chair. When he was comfortably settled she dropped down to her haunches again to check his knee and the protective cast for any new signs of damage. *Thankfully she couldn't find any.* She'd had the most awful fright when she saw that he'd fallen over, and she couldn't forgive herself for allowing him to persuade her to go and make a drink rather than stay with him as she should have done. She would never make the same mistake again, she vowed.

Glancing up, she witnessed a muscle visibly flinch in the side of his lean shadowed jaw. 'Everything looks okay but that doesn't mean you haven't damaged anything,' she said. 'Can you raise your injured leg off the floor a little for me, so that I can ascertain how much movement you've got?'

He did so with a rueful smile. Nothing appeared amiss, and Kit was temporarily able to relax. Rising to her feet, she resisted the sudden shocking impulse to comb his hair back from his forehead with her fingers. For goodness' sake! He wasn't a child! *But there'd been nothing remotely maternal about her urge to touch the dark silken locks.*

All the while she'd been helping him into the bath, washing his hair, then helping him out again, her senses had been taunted and aroused by his dangerously irresistible maleness and close proximity. The scent of his cologne along with the dizzying warmth of his body, seemed still to cling to her. Her very cells felt as though they'd been imbued with his essence. Not to mention the thrill of that brief kiss they'd shared...

In a bid to ground herself, she sucked in a steadying breath. 'I saw in the diary that the nurse is calling in tomorrow. That's good. I'll feel more reassured when she checks you over.'

'Worried about me, are you, Ms Blessington?'

The teasing glimmer in his compelling golden eyes reassured her that perhaps it *had* been only his pride that had been hurt. In any case, she wouldn't let herself rest on her laurels.

'Don't take it personally. I'd be worried about anyone in my care who had fallen over—especially someone who already has a broken leg. But you can be sure that next time I won't be so quick to believe you when you tell me you can manage on your own. That was an unforgivable mistake I made. If you want that hot drink I'll help you into the kitchen so that you can sit at the table with me. Then I think you should seriously consider going to bed.'

'That would sound like a much more attractive proposition if I didn't have to go there alone.'

Hal's huskily voiced statement—its meaning all too clear—nailed Kit's feet to the floor. The shock that eddied through her was so strong it made her feel dizzy.

Over a dry mouth, she answered, 'Is that so? Look, what you do in your private life is none of my business, but I'd urge you to give your body a chance to heal a bit more before you—before you—'

'Before I attend to needs of a more...shall we say... *personal* nature?'

After holding her stunned gaze for what seemed like a heart-pounding lifetime, with a wry twist of his lips he suddenly grimaced and shook his head.

'You're right, of course. But then it seems that you always *are*, Kit. I'd like to have a talk with you about how you came to be so eminently sensible. But right now I'm too tired, so our little chat will have to wait until tomorrow.'

Her acute discomfort at his previous incendiary comment thankfully easing, Kit collected Hal's walking aid and helped him get to his feet again. Once she was satisfied that he had his balance she walked by his side out into the corridor, then accompanied him into the kitchen...

CHAPTER FIVE

IT WAS IMPOSSIBLE to drift off into a relaxed sleep after the day's events—events that had upsettingly culminated in Hal's shocking fall. Kit thanked her lucky stars that he hadn't injured himself more, but she was still anxious to have the nurse check him over when she visited tomorrow. She prayed the woman wouldn't think she hadn't done her job properly because she'd left Hal unsupervised and in doing so proved herself incompetent. The last thing Kit wanted was to have her report back to Hal's sister with the suggestion that she hire someone else. It would be the first black mark on her unblemished record with the agency if she did.

Unable to banish the worry and doubt that plagued her, she thumped the luxurious feather pillow she'd been resting her head on and turned over onto her side. Her mind raced on. More than anything else she wanted Hal Treverne to see that she was the very best at what she did, and for him to realise that she was totally dedicated to helping aid his recovery.

Is that all you want him to see? That you're competent and good at what you do?

'Oh, for goodness' sake.'

Once more Kit sat up and drove her fingers restlessly

through her hair. The provoking question her mind had mocked her with was hardly conducive to her getting much sleep at all that night if she decided to explore it, she realised. *Yet she couldn't deny that the man disturbed her.* He made her more aware of her femininity than any other man had ever done before…especially when he kissed her!

The fact that he had a broken leg and was irritable and frustrated by his resultant immobility didn't make Kit any less aware of the man's undoubted charisma and sex appeal. But then, when she recalled that Hal had told her at the interview that he might need to call on her for company at night if he couldn't sleep, her heart skipped an anxious beat. People were apt to let their guard down more during the night-time hours. What would they talk about? Kit wouldn't dream of betraying any confidences he might share, but at the same time she hoped he wouldn't expect her to reveal any of her own. She'd never been at all easy talking about her past, and whenever it arose she'd developed a strategy of automatically glossing over the details and then acting as if it was hardly of any consequence.

'The past is in the past and that's where it should stay,' she'd comment, endeavouring for a blithe, cheery tone.

Would Hal Treverne break her cover and intuit that her guard was as strong as a portcullis slamming down to keep out the enemy if he should veer into that particular territory? And would he wonder why she was so reluctant to talk about it? Only tonight he'd vowed to talk to her about what had made her 'so eminently sensible' she recalled. His resolution had made her understandably anxious at the idea of even *briefly* having to revisit the circumstances and events that had shaped her. To discuss her past with him might threaten to open a can of worms that wouldn't easily be closed… It could also undo the self-confidence she'd built up over the past few years since working for the agency. *It might even destroy it completely.*

Making an abrupt decision to deal with whatever should transpire and not allow it to make her flustered, Kit resignedly combed her fingers through her freed mane of silken copper hair once again and lay back down. Deciding to draw upon the sheer determination and pragmatism she usually utilised to get her through life's challenges, she promised herself she would have a far less troubling day tomorrow, come what may. And on that reassuring note she finally allowed her eyes to drift closed…

The surprising realisation that hit Hal on opening his eyes the next morning was that for the first time since the accident he had astonishingly experienced an unbroken night's sleep. He'd slept through the night without waking even once. Barely able to believe it, he sat upright, bemusedly scrubbed his hand round his studded jaw and then pushed back the duvet. Yes, he'd taken two strong painkillers before retiring, but they had never worked as effectively before.

Had his redheaded guardian angel put some kind of spell on him? Glancing down at his injured leg, he saw that even the swelling on his damaged knee had diminished a little. That stupid fall of his last night hadn't hurt him at all. But it *had* acted as a warning to him not to refuse Kit's help when he needed it all because he was striving to be so damn independent! From now on he would endeavour to be more sensible. His swift recovery so that he could return to his busy life *depended* on it.

Although he had a bevy of reliable people working for him, he wouldn't be happy until he was back at the helm overseeing things and feeling satisfied that everything was being done properly and to the high standards he expected.

A short while after he had washed and dressed there was a knock on the door and his intention to be sensible was immediately put to the test as Kit came in, pushing his wheelchair. This morning she was wearing mouth-wateringly fitted blue jeans that hugged her slender hips and thighs as though paying devoted homage to her arresting contours and what looked to be a large-sized man's red and white check flannel shirt, encircled by a shiny red belt that showed off her ridiculously small waist. Once again her wavy auburn hair was threatening to tumble free from the topknot that never seemed quite able to secure it.

Hal stared. He couldn't help it. A bolt of white-hot heat shot through him at the thought of taking down that fiery hair, unbuttoning the ridiculous man's shirt she wore, freeing her breasts from her bra and kissing them until his lips and body were on fire from the sea of blissful pleasure that he would no doubt be drowning in…

'Good morning.' She smiled.

Feeling somewhat dazed by his heated reaction at seeing her again, Hal continued to make a personal inventory of her assets as though noticing them for the very first time. Her eyes were as blue as the brightest delphiniums that Mother Nature could devise, and her rosy cheeks and full red lips would surely tempt even the most devout monk to rethink his vows. Kissing them would be like tasting the sweetest ripe cherries he could imagine.

'Henry...are you all right?'

The most exquisite little frown he had ever seen puckered Kit's smooth alabaster brow. She *must* have put a spell on him. He had a creative mind, but never before in his entire romantic history to date had he thought of a woman's frown as being 'exquisite'. He sat on the edge of the vast king-sized bed, with his injured leg stretched out in front of him and resting on a footstool, and right then life felt surprisingly good. If this was what this incredible woman could do for him—make him feel happy to be alive in the midst of what he had previously deemed a *disaster*—then he'd be an absolute idiot to let her go.

At last he managed to convey his pleasure at seeing her to his lips. Shaping them into a pleased smile, he said, 'I'm absolutely fine. In fact I've never felt better.'

'I take it you're being sardonic?' Again Kit frowned, but this time the gesture was undoubtedly more perturbed.

'Not at all. I slept like a baby last night. Consequently I feel on top of the world.'

'Must have been those painkillers that you took.'

'Maybe.' With his smile still intact, Hal nonchalantly shrugged his big shoulders.

With a bemused sigh Kit manoeuvred the wheelchair a little closer towards him. 'Anyway...I thought I'd wheel you into the kitchen for breakfast this morning and save the wear and tear on your legs. Especially after that fall you had last night. You can use your crutches later, after you've seen the nurse and when you've rested up a bit.'

Even though her concerned declaration made Hal feel more like an eighty-year-old than a young, fit man at the height of his powers—or at least he *had been* until his accident—he was predisposed to forgive her, because the very welcome sleep he'd enjoyed last night, along with the growing realisation that she was somehow becoming important to him, made him feel much more amiable than he'd felt in a very long while. But he couldn't resist the opportunity to gently make fun of her. 'Save the wear and tear on my legs? Who was your last client, Kit? *Methuselah*?'

'Very funny. Why don't you get into the wheelchair and we'll go and get you some breakfast before the nurse arrives?'

At the table, Kit poured him a large mug of coffee and then sat opposite him to sip the cup of tea she'd made for herself.

'I'm so relieved to hear that you slept well last night,' she told him. 'I was worried that your fall might have given you a few extra aches and pains to keep you awake.'

'Well, it didn't. Like I said, I slept like a baby. By the way, what time is the nurse due?'

'I checked in the diary and she'll be here in about an hour. That gives me plenty of time to get you your breakfast. What can I get for you?'

'A couple of slices of wholemeal toast with marmalade will suffice. I rarely have much more than that.'

'Well…' Her rosy cheeks dimpled disarmingly. 'One of these mornings I'm hoping you'll let me cook you the full English. It's one of my specialties.'

Fielding another bolt of disturbing heat, because he'd realised how more and more attractive she was becoming to him, Hal leveled her a deliberately flirtatious smile. 'How could I refuse such an irresistible invitation? You certainly know how to tempt a man when he's down, Ms Blessington...especially when he's literally been knocked off his feet.'

His companion's even white teeth worried delicately at her fulsome lower lip.

'Are you saying that you're more susceptible to temptation when you're feeling low?'

Hal responded with a short, ironic laugh. 'I hardly need a reason to be more susceptible to temptation than I am already.' His voice had turned unwittingly husky and Kit's rosy cheeks turned even rosier, he noticed.

'Well...' Seizing the chance to free herself from his undoubtedly disconcerting examination, she got hurriedly to her feet. 'I'd better get on with making you that toast.'

'Don't forget to do some for yourself.'

'All I need in the morning is a cup of tea.'

His gaze swept pointedly up and down her figure. 'You'll fade away. You're not on some ridiculous diet, I hope?'

'No, I'm not.' Her expression was painfully affronted. 'Do you think I'd be on a diet at the expense of my health? I trust I have more common sense than that. In any case I'm a high-energy person and I don't easily put on weight. The more I do, the more I just burn it off.'

'Well, don't get too skinny.' Hal grinned, absent-mindedly stirring another teaspoon of sugar into his coffee. 'I like my women to have a decent amount of flesh on their bones.'

'Well...how fortunate that I'm not one of your women, then,' Kit returned smartly, delphinium-blue eyes flashing. 'In any case, according to the press, you certainly have plenty to choose from.'

So she *had* read those tiresome reports of his so-called salacious conduct in the newspapers. It seemed he wasn't going to get off lightly in her eyes...broken leg or no broken leg. She wouldn't be in a hurry to grant him any kind of dispensation. He silently balked at the idea that what she'd read about him might have already sullied her opinion.

'It may or may not interest you to know, but I haven't had a date in over six months now—and you really should be a bit more discerning about what you read in the tabloids, Kit. Maybe it's time you changed to a better class of newspaper?'

The flush on her face was akin to the shade of fresh beetroot, and Hal instantly regretted the biting comment. But it was too late to retract it.

'You're entitled to your opinion, of course. Would you like some more coffee with your toast, Mr Treverne?'

Moving over to the shiny stainless steel toaster on the counter, Kit had obviously decided not to get into a debate about the issue, and although he secretly craved her forgiveness for being so cutting Hal was undeniably relieved. *But he still wasn't able to let her have the last word...*

'So we're back to the more formal address now, are we? I told you I'd prefer it if you didn't call me that. Anyway...'

She turned just in time to see him raise a mocking eyebrow, his gaze unwavering and direct.

'…don't you think it's rather ridiculous when you've seen me buck naked in the bath?'

'You had a towel wrapped round you, as I recall.' Kit crossed her arms over her shirt and her glance was formidably fierce.

'A ridiculously *small* towel that left very little to the imagination, I'm sure.'

'Are you forgetting that I helped you into your robe afterwards?'

'No, I hadn't forgotten. I was merely being a gentleman and not mentioning it.'

With a bemused look, Kit sighed. 'At any rate, don't you think I have anything better to do than spend my time dwelling on what you look like naked?'

'No doubt you do. But don't bruise my already fragile ego by denying me the very healthy male fantasy of you lusting after my body in your spare time.'

'Oh, for goodness' sake…you're impossible!'

'I've been called worse things in my time.'

'I think we should just call a halt to this inane conversation right now and concentrate on having our breakfast, don't you?'

Once again Hal lifted a sardonic brow. 'You just told me that you don't eat breakfast.'

With a frustrated groan, Kit pushed back the tendril of auburn hair that had drifted onto her forehead and exasperatedly rolled her eyes. 'Well, I might just be driven to it to help me keep up my strength if you persist in trying to wind me up all day!'

It was perverse, but Hal privately admitted to a strange delight in knowing he could get to her—even if her reaction wasn't the usual smitten one he'd grown used to receiving from women.

Taking a couple of satisfying sips of his coffee, he gave her a disarming grin. 'I'll do my best not to aggravate you, sweetheart, really I will. But you surely can't deny a poor invalid these only too brief opportunities to brighten up his day? That is not unless you have a heart of stone?'

'So it's a "poor invalid" you are now, is it?'

'What else could I be when I'm stuck here in this wheelchair?' Suddenly, out of the blue, his mood turning on a sixpence, Hal's frustration at his immobility got the better of him. 'Trust me, angel. If I wasn't so incapacitated by this blasted broken leg I'd be chasing you round the room until I caught you and stole a long, satisfying kiss!' The very idea at being able to carry out such a threat instantly restored his good humour. 'Although I know *one* could never possibly be enough.'

'Don't you remember you already stole one yesterday?'

'You told me you'd forgotten about that. Maybe it left more of an impression than you admitted? Perhaps I should take a chance and steal another one to remind you how good it was?'

'I don't agree. Although I won't deny you your harmless little fantasy if it helps to keep your spirits up. Anything that aids your recovery is fine by me, because once you're up and about again, and you can get back to your busy life and the no doubt infinite number of women who find you so irresistible, you'll be a lot happier and my job here will be done.'

Just before she turned away to slot some bread into the toaster Hal saw her lips wrestle with the most maddening grin and he couldn't help scowling because—unbelievably—she had bettered him by finally getting the last word…

Having pronounced him better than she'd hoped, the cheerful nurse from the private hospital Hal attended departed, promising to see him again in a week's time and instructing him to call if he needed to see her sooner. When she'd gone he told Kit that he intended to work in his study until lunchtime and that she could please herself what she did until then.

Cutting him down to size with the comments she'd made in the kitchen before the nurse arrived had made her regret being so outspoken, because since then he'd fallen worryingly silent and there had been no more provocative banter between them. Even though her blood had throbbed like honey heated over a slow-burning flame when Hal had confessed he wished he could chase her round the room and steal another kiss…

Kit knew she shouldn't encourage any more flirtatious comments because it would only make it harder not to see him again when her job came to an end. Besides, she knew he couldn't possibly be serious about wanting to kiss her for a second time. She was certain that the brief but delicious kiss he'd delivered yesterday had only come about because the circumstances had been so helplessly intimate. After all, you couldn't get much more intimate than helping a man into the bath and washing his hair, Kit reflected, her blood heating at the memory.

Besides, according to the press, he'd dated some of the most beautiful women in the world. There was no way on God's good green earth that Kit could ever hope to match up to any of them…but then nor would she want to. *If* she ever fell in love with someone it would have to be with a man who wasn't so easily seduced by the temptations of the world, or one who felt he had to keep up some kind of glossy 'action man' image to be accepted by it.

No…none of that would be necessary, because the man she settled on would soon learn that he was with a woman who truly loved him for himself…*not* for what he could achieve or provide materially. Biting her lip, because she'd been drawn into mulling over a scenario that she rarely allowed herself to dwell on, Kit started in surprise when five minutes later Hal called her into his study.

After knocking and entering the room, Kit stared wide-eyed at the proudly displayed evidence of his achievement—awards he'd received from the music industry and stunning photographs of the various sporting challenges he'd participated in round the world. The only evidence of anything more personal was a lovely silver-framed portrait of his sister Sam.

Unable to help herself, Kit twitched her lips in amusement when her glance collided with the calendar above Hal's desk. The photograph depicting the current month *was* of a generously curved, famous blonde model wearing a white bikini… Scratch that… *Nearly* wearing a white bikini. She was still smiling when her gaze returned to Hal and saw that his chameleon-gold eyes were studying her intently, as if he was wondering what she made of all the awards and pictures on show… *never mind the audacious calendar*.

'You must be very proud of all your achievements,' she commented brightly. She didn't anticipate the downturned mouth and impatient shrug he gave her in response.

'There are other things I'd like to achieve more,' he answered intriguingly.

'Like what, exactly?'

The handsome features were instantly guarded. 'It's not something I feel inclined to discuss right now, if you don't mind.'

'I don't mind at all.'

Kit genuinely meant that, but she couldn't help but be curious as to what exactly Hal Treverne wanted to achieve that was even more commendable than what he'd attained already. Was there any goal or pursuit in the privileged world he inhabited that he *hadn't* accomplished or excelled at? *It didn't seem likely.*

Lightly folding her arms over her flannel shirt, she asked, 'What did you call me in for?'

Leaning back in his leather chair, he extracted a business card from his leather wallet and handed it to her.

'I'd like you to book a table for two at this restaurant for lunch today. Tell them that I'd like one of the more private tables, with some space around it so that I can stretch out my leg.'

Briefly examining the card and recognising the name of an elite Michelin-starred restaurant that the rich and famous were known to frequent, Kit quickly scanned her memory banks for easily accessible nearby parking in the area.

As if reading her mind, Hal said, 'You don't have to worry about parking. The concierge will have a member of staff do that for us when we arrive.'

'Okay. What time should I book the table for?'

'Half past one will be fine.'

'And are you meeting your guest at the restaurant?' Her heart thudded heavily at the thought that he was probably meeting some nubile blonde who was his latest lady-friend. Kit didn't quite buy his assertion that he hadn't dated in over six months. A man like Hal Treverne wouldn't be without a woman for very long—not if his colourful reputation was anything to go by.

'What guest?' He was looking distinctly perplexed. 'It's *you* I'm going to lunch with, Kit. Isn't that obvious?'

Now her heart thudded even harder. 'But you're booking a table at one of the most fashionable eateries in town. Do I have to dress up? If I do then I can't go. My wardrobe doesn't stretch to anything remotely suitable for a restaurant like that, and I don't want to embarrass you.'

'Embarrass me? You obviously don't get out a lot do you, sweetheart?' Tunnelling his fingers through his thick mane of dark curls, Hal shook his head bemusedly. 'You don't need fashionable clothing, or indeed any adornment other than that mane of glorious fiery hair and those beautiful blue eyes of yours, to make you fit to appear in any fancy restaurant in the world. Besides, I've frequented this particular establishment more times than I care to mention, and trust me…' the sculpted lips shaped themselves into an irrepressible grin '…the owner—who happens to be a personal friend of mine—would cut off his right arm rather than risk losing my custom.'

Silently reeling from the totally unexpected effusive compliment she'd just received, and the fact that yet again he had called her sweetheart, Kit struggled for a moment to reply.

'All right, then. I'll go ahead and make the reservation.'

'Good. Now, as much as I regret bringing our little tête-à-tête' to an end, I suppose I'd better get on with some work. By the way, Mrs Baker, my cleaning lady, is due in soon. Let her in and introduce yourself, will you?'

'Of course.'

'Good.'

As he turned his attention back to the paperwork strewn untidily across his desk Kit quietly let herself out, wondering what she could do to help make her more impervious to Hal Treverne's irresistible charm and charisma if she were to continue to stay working for him.

CHAPTER SIX

IN ADMIRATION, HAL had seen Kit turn what might have been a somewhat awkward entrance into the restaurant into a flawlessly smooth operation that he could never have managed on his own. Even though he was well-known, and it had no doubt not gone unnoticed by the other notable diners that he'd been injured in a foolish skiing accident, Hal hated the idea of inviting unnecessary attention when all he wanted to do was enjoy some of the finest cuisine in the country in peace with his chosen companion.

But even when he'd happened to catch someone's inquisitive gaze Kit's gracious smile and softly spoken reassuring words at his side had helped him to brush it off and they had proceeded to their table unhindered.

Pleased that his confidence in walking with the aids was definitely improving, Hal relaxed. His spirits rose even more when he saw that it was his beautiful Titian-haired companion who was drawing most of the attentive glances that came their way—he certainly wasn't above feeling some typically masculine pride at having an attractive companion.

The interest in Kit had started with the charming French *maître d'*, who had all but gone into Gallic ecstasy at the sight of her rippling burnished hair. She wore it loose at Hal's request, because he'd wanted to see it unbound again. And it hadn't been hard to detect the curious minds of the other diners avidly whirring at their entrance into the restaurant. They must be wondering about their relationship, putting two and two together and undoubtedly making five...

But whatever people were imagining about his association with Kit Hal couldn't deny that his idea of making their relationship more intimate had been growing stronger the more time they spent together, and he longed to make it a reality.

'Can I tempt you with some wine?' he asked as Kit's extraordinary blue eyes gravely studied her copy of the leather-bound menu.

'Wine?' She blinked up at him in astonishment. 'I'm driving. Did you forget?'

Unbelievably, he *had*. He was so lost in his contemplation of her captivating features that it seemed he had forgotten how to think straight. Embarrassed heat pulsed through his bloodstream and he knew it must have invaded his face. The atypical reaction made him feel like an inexperienced schoolboy instead of a thirty-two-year-old man who had always been supremely confident around women... *It was hardly a feeling he welcomed.*

'I confess I did. It's a shame. They have some incredible wine here.' Lifting his own copy of the menu, he attempted to peruse it.

Taking him by surprise, Kit leaned across and curled her elegantly slim hand round his.

'It doesn't mean that you shouldn't have a glass if

you want one. Although I'd advise you not to overdo it since you're taking medication at the moment.'

Hal hardly registered her words because the touch of her skin against his was like receiving an electric shock that left him reeling. Now he didn't just *like* her touch, he realised…he had begun avidly to *crave* it. But as his heartbeat slowly started to return to its normal rhythm he couldn't deny that she'd pricked his pride by reminding him of his current despised condition.

'I might have known my personal guardian angel would remind me of that fact. How fortunate that you always seem to be here when I need you, Kit.'

She instantly withdrew her hand. *He might have slapped her face.*

'That's what you're paying me for, isn't it…? To be a help to you while you recuperate?' She made a show of being interested in the menu again but her gaze returned almost immediately to examine him. 'If you don't like the way I'm doing my job perhaps you'd be happier with someone else?'

'Don't do this. Not here.' Lowering his voice, Hal glanced briefly across the packed restaurant. Then, leaning towards her with a frown, he said, 'It might be interpreted that we're having a personal relationship and it's not going very well. I don't want anyone getting the wrong impression and for a story to find its way into the tabloids so they can belittle me like they usually do.'

Her alabaster complexion flushed cerise and he realised he could have chosen his words a lot more carefully.

'What do you mean by the wrong impression? I'm nobody,' Kit demanded softly. 'It's not as if I'm your wife or girlfriend. Who cares what anyone else thinks?'

'*I* do.' He swallowed hard. It was impossible to tear his gaze away because he was mortified to think that he'd insulted her...*hurt* her, even. If he had, then he had a profound desire to make things right again. 'And I didn't mean to imply that it bothers me if people think our relationship is personal. Did you think it would? You sell yourself short if you do. You're a very beautiful woman, Kit, and it wouldn't be beyond anyone's understanding if I was attracted to you.'

'Now it's *my* turn to ask you not to do this. I'd prefer it if we both remembered why I'm here and didn't lose sight of that in some pointless, ridiculous fantasy.'

Self-consciously she'd lowered her voice, but the pink flush on her cheeks rendered her so irresistibly pretty that Hal didn't think twice about reaching out his hand to gently stroke his fingertips across her cheek.

Kit bit down on her lip as though pained. 'Don't. The waiter's coming towards us and we haven't even discussed what we're going to eat yet.'

'I heartily recommend the herb-crusted lamb. Trust me—what they do with it is close to *orgasmic*.' Grinning, Hal kissed his fingers with a deliberately theatrical flourish.

Kit had just about recovered her composure in time, he saw, as the waiter appeared to ask smilingly if they'd made their selection. Giving Hal the barest warning glance, she unhesitatingly went for the lamb. Despite the warning, he couldn't resist giving her a teasing wink of acknowledgment that she'd taken him at his word and succumbed to his enthusiastic recommendation without a murmur. He took it as a good sign that she trusted him.

'Well, well, well! I see the walking wounded has returned to the land of the living, looking as disgustingly handsome and fit as ever…despite the broken leg!'

Hal was seriously starting to relax and enjoy Kit's company, as well as his indisputably delicious meal, when a familiar male voice sent a disagreeable chill down his back. Looking up, he came face to face with the insincere smile of his ex-business partner Simon Rigden.

Simon was wearing his trademark designer suit, and his mid-brown hair was slicked back and as perfectly styled as always. But his over-familiar air and polished appearance weren't about to make Hal feel remotely friendly or predisposed to let bygones be bygones. The man was a wily snake and he'd be a fool to forget that for a second time. The pity was that he hadn't recognised it as being the case when they'd first met and he had stupidly made him his partner…

Ignoring the slightly pudgy hand held out before him in greeting, he took his time in touching his linen napkin to his lips, then emitted a weary sigh. 'If your aim was to ruin my day by appearing like this then you're wasting your time, Simon. That skiing accident on the Aspen slopes confirmed the realisation I already had about you…of what a conniving, merciless little weasel you are.'

Glancing across the restaurant, Hal saw a couple of similarly dressed businessmen he didn't know from Adam raise their glasses to him in a presumptuous gesture of acknowledgement. Clearly his one-time friend and business partner had company—and perhaps not so *savoury* company.

'Why don't you just slink back to what I'm sure are your equally disagreeable companions and endeavour to ruin their day instead? I have every confidence you'll more than succeed.'

Beneath the tan that he liked to keep topped up with frequent trips to the Caribbean and other fashionable hot spots round the world, Simon visibly flushed. But then exerting a little sweat and doing an honest day's work had never been one of his biggest priorities, Hal recalled. It was one of the reasons he had paid him off—in hindsight far too generously—and brought their partnership to an end. In another era Simon Rigden would have been known as being a reprehensible *louche,* he was certain.

'You're obviously feeling bitter because I won our little bet that I was a better skier than you and that I could beat you on what's known to be one of the most challenging slopes in the world,' Simon accused him mockingly. 'You feel humiliated that you crashed into that snowbank in front of several of your cronies. Everyone knows how much you hate to lose, but you weren't exactly "Lucky Henry" that day—were you, Hal?'

'You'd better leave before I signal the *maître d'* and have you thrown out for being a nuisance.'

'And risk having your reckless reputation highlighted once again in the tabloids? Although I'll concede this restaurant *does* make an admirable effort to keep out the riff-raff, one or two hacks always manage to sneak under the radar. See any faces you don't recognise?'

Hal bristled. 'Why don't you just get out of *my* face and leave me and my companion to enjoy our lunch in peace?'

The other man's gaze swung interestedly across the table to Kit.

'And who might *you* be, sweetheart? I must say I'm

surprised. I thought our friend's preference was for voluptuous blondes—not dainty little redheads who look like they come straight out of the Renaissance. But I suppose you must possess one or two sexy little tricks to keep him keen. You'll certainly need to invent a few more of those if you're going to keep him happy whilst he's immobile. I hear it was a particularly bad break, and my guess is his recuperation is going to be a long one. But if his interest starts to wane at any time, sweetheart, you should give me a call.'

His pudgy hand dived into his wallet to extract a business card. He threw it down in front of Kit in a gesture clearly meant to insult. 'I've had my surfeit of blondes lately, and I must admit, I could use a change.'

The look on Hal's face would have put the fear of God into a man with any modicum of sensitivity.

'Carry on in that vein, Rigden,' he warned, 'and I swear you'll live to regret it. Now, get out of my sight! You're not fit to even *look* at her. In fact you'd better get out of here quick—before I call the police.'

'It's all right, Henry. I can deal with this.' Calmly taking a sip of her orange juice, with both men staring at her in mute fascination, Kit followed up this remark with another confident assertion. 'I'd rather take my chances in a pool of piranhas than waste even a second of my time on an unsavoury character like you, Mr… er…?' Coolly she picked up the business card that had been so insultingly flung down in front of her and read the name on it out loud. *'Mr Simon Rigden.'* Pinning him with a direct and frosty glare, she finished, 'You can be sure I'll remember that, if I'm ever interviewed as a witness when Mr Treverne takes you to court on a charge of harassment. One thing's for sure—it won't enhance your reputation.'

'*Touché,*' Hal murmured beneath his breath.

'You little—' Flushing, the businessman abruptly turned on his heel and promptly left the restaurant, not even troubling to return to his companions and explain the reason he was leaving.

Given the looks of resignation on their faces, Hal deduced they weren't at all surprised by his sudden exit. Some people just had a knack for self-sabotage...

Immediately returning his gaze to the much more pleasing sight of his Titian-haired companion, he asked, 'What made you do that?'

'You mean cut him down to size and stand up for myself?'

'Yes.'

Kit's blue eyes flashed. 'Let's just say I've had plenty of experience in dealing with men like him. My mother brought men like Simon Rigden home with monotonous and painful regularity in her search for the man of her dreams. Needless to say it was a fruitless and soul-destroying exercise. Unfailingly, her dreams turned into a nightmare. She wasn't the best judge of men. And when each of those men took what they wanted and then abandoned her—which they did, without exception—I was the one left to pick up the pieces and try and convince her that what didn't kill her would make her stronger. Except that it never did...' Her gaze looked far away for a moment. 'Make her stronger, I mean...'

'That must have left some scars on you,' Hal remarked, expressing the compassion he was feeling that she'd endured such a horrendous experience. It explained a lot about why she was so guarded and self-contained, so determined to protect herself from similar predators.

Grimacing, Kit gave a brief shake of her head. Her blue eyes were like the most intense moonlit stars they were so bright.

'Scars heal…but unfortunately memories don't. But you were right…that Rigden chap really *is* a weasel. What decent, right-minded man would mock a friend because he had lost a bet and suffered serious injury? It's clear he doesn't have any principles. It's none of my business, and I don't mean to be presumptuous, but I'd steer clear of him in the future, if I were you.'

'Trust me. I *will*. I only wish I'd known the low-life was going to be dining here today—I would have suggested we went somewhere else. He keeps trying to rile me because he's still mad that I broke off our partnership.'

'So *he's* your ex-business partner? If you don't mind my asking, what on earth made you go into business with someone like him?'

'Ever heard the saying that a salesman can always be sold to?' Shrugging his shoulders, Hal was still pained to admit he'd been so gullible. 'I was in my early twenties when he approached me, having heard about the success I'd been having, and I was eager to prove to my father that I could do even better. So when Simon offered me what sounded like a good deal at the time I suppose I let down my usual guard and fell for his convincing spiel. He was an experienced businessman in the industry that interested me the most, and his record of success was impressive.'

He gave a wry grimace.

'Anyway, getting back to the skiing incident, when I saw him on the slopes at Aspen the only reason I agreed

to his stupid bet was because I was certain I could beat
him. I'd never lost a similar challenge before. But the
truth is I was an egotistical idiot and I paid the price. I
should have just walked away. But I want to sincerely
apologise for Rigden's insulting you, Kit. If I were back
on my feet *he* would have been the one who was immobilised.'

The comment clearly perturbed her.

'I can understand the impulse, but I abhor violence.
It doesn't solve anything in my view. Doesn't the fact
that there are so many wars in the world tell you that?
It would be much better to talk things out or simply just
ignore him. That would wound him more.'

An amused quirk lifted a corner of his lips. 'Well, the
fact that you made it clear you weren't interested and
then warned him what might happen if he continued
to make a nuisance of himself was more than enough
to see him off. You were quite formidable in your defence of me, Kit. I'm seriously impressed. The only
other person who would have been quite so protective
is my sister Sam.'

Giving him a captivating smile, Kit picked up the
pristine silver cutlery she had laid at the side of her
dinner plate 'I'll take that as a compliment. But now I
think we should finish eating our meal before it gets
cold, don't you?'

'I can always get the waiter to bring us fresh food
if need be.'

'And waste all that money you're paying for what
we've got already? No chance!'

Kit was deeply reflective on their return to the apartment. The appearance of Simon Rigden at the restaurant
had given her a graphic insight into Hal's regret about

going into partnership with such a man. *'A salesman can always be sold to,'* he'd said drolly. One thing was certain: she was sure he'd never be sold to by such a merciless shark again.

Walking beside him over to the couch, where he carefully lowered himself onto the firm leather seats and handed her his walking aids, Kit noticed that he looked particularly tired—as if the outing had been more of a strain than he wanted to let on. Not only had it been his first visit to a restaurant since his accident but, along with negotiating the challenge of appearing in public again when he wasn't as fit as he wanted to be, he had been confronted by the one person who was *guaranteed* to raise his stress levels… Kit hoped it wouldn't set his recovery back in any way.

Intermingled with those thoughts was the memory of telling Hal about her mother and her history of failed relationships due to her poor choice of men. Would she have revealed something so personal if Simon Rigden hadn't presented himself at their table to mock him?

'I'm going to relax for a while. Why don't you take the opportunity to do the same?'

Hal broke into her reverie with a beguiling smile. Was the man aware that if that smile were flashed up on a cinema screen it would have every woman and girl in the vicinity aching with longing for an opportunity to be intimately acquainted with him? Her body warmed helplessly. For Kit it was a new experience to be so acutely aware of a man…to the point where almost every other thought in her head evaporated when he directed that chameleon golden-eyed glance at her.

'Later on this evening I thought we could watch a

couple of movies together and afterwards have a talk about them?'

He settled back against the plumped-up cushions on the couch with his hands behind his head, which had the disconcerting result of drawing her gaze to the impressive muscular chest so lovingly hugged by his black cashmere sweater.

Her mouth nervously dried as he added, 'Are you up for that? And don't you dare tell me it's what I'm paying you for.'

'I'd love to do that…watch a couple of movies with you, I mean. But I think that I'll pass on your suggestion to relax. I know that Mrs Baker has been in today to clean the house, but I'd like to check if there's anything else that needs doing and if we need any supplies from the supermarket. If you're resting, it would be a good opportunity. I know you probably won't like me for saying it, but you're not paying me to be idle. Besides, I like to keep busy and do what I can to make things a little easier for my clients. Talking of which…' Kit couldn't resist smiling '…I'd like to ice that leg for you at some point and check that everything's okay.'

'Everything's fine.' Hal moved his hands from behind his head to drive his fingers a tad irritably through his dark hair. 'I'd tell you if it wasn't…*Nurse* Blessington.'

Kit feigned a disapproving look. 'I don't profess to be a nurse, but I know what has to be done and how to do it, so I don't mind if you think I'm a little bossy. Anyway, you should rest now. Just behave yourself while I'm gone,' she chided, 'and don't do anything you shouldn't.'

'Really?' he mocked. The devastating glint in his eye made her legs turn to mush. 'Like what, for instance?'

Flustered, she hurried across to the door and opened it. 'Oh, I don't know… Abseiling out of the window, perhaps? One thing's for sure: if there's any mischief to be found you're just the man to find it…intrepid thrill-seeker that you are!'

His delighted laughter followed her all the way down the hall and into the kitchen…

CHAPTER SEVEN

AT HAL'S INVITATION, Kit sat next to him on the couch as they watched the first film, making sure to leave a decent amount of space between them. But he had dimmed the lights, and even though the film's story was engrossing she couldn't relax because of her heightened awareness of everything about him.

Not that he had to rely on anything external to enhance his undoubted appeal, but did he *have* to wear such a provocatively arresting aftershave? The scent was seriously taunting her and after having experienced his kiss in the bathroom—albeit a too brief one—she could hardly think about much else other than sex! The thrill of his unexpected caress had seriously excited her, and it didn't help that she hadn't known a man's touch since the only other man she had gone to bed with had turned out to be a liar and a cheat.

The celibacy she'd imposed on herself since that episode had never backfired on her in such a disturbing and inconvenient way before. It surely wasn't the brightest idea she'd ever had to lust after her boss, even though Hal Treverne was pretty impossible to resist!

Clearing her throat, she absently curled a long strand of her burnished copper hair round her finger.

'Are you okay?'

Turning her head at the question, Kit curved her lips in an automatic smile. 'Yes, I'm fine.'

Her quick-fire reply was hasty and unsure, and the smile that accompanied it was by no means meant to be invitational or provocative, but her companion's arresting golden eyes darkened visibly in response. He also shifted in his seat, as though suddenly uncomfortable with his position. One thing was immediately clear. *He was in no hurry to get back to the film.*

'Is it me or has it got seriously hot in here?' he commented.

Over the slow and heavy thud of her heartbeat Kit tried her best to think straight. 'It *is* quite warm,' she agreed. 'Perhaps I should turn the heating down a little?'

'It won't make any difference.'

Her companion's lips shaped a compellingly wry grin that displayed his perfectly even white teeth and once again made Kit think he ought to be in the movies. But right then, in this dimly lit state-of-the-art modern living room, she was very glad that he wasn't. She had no desire to share him with anyone…let alone the whole world.

'Well, then, I suppose we'd better just watch the movie.'

Glancing away, she attempted to focus on the large screen facing her instead of on Hal, in a bid to not to be so distracted by him. But he was right. It *was* hot in here—and it wasn't just down to the very efficient heating system.

'Kit?'

'Yes?'

'Why don't you move a little nearer? It's a big couch and it feels like you're miles away.'

'Why do you need me to move nearer? Are you in pain? Shall I get your medication?'

In answer his golden eyes transmitted the kind of simmering heat reserved for burning embers, and the raw, impassioned hunger Kit saw reflected there was impossible to ignore. Her slender thighs, clad in black leggings beneath a matching roomy sweater, clenched defensively together. But in truth she knew she was on a hiding to nothing. A shiver convulsed her slender frame. If she hoped to be able to ride out the merciless electric storm confronting her, then it was already clear she was odds-on to lose.

'I'm not in pain, but if I was the only thing that would help ease it is *you*, Kit.'

Her eyes widening, she replied tremulously, 'Don't say that—at least not in that way. You hired me to work for you. Nothing else. I would never jeopardise my job by—by…' Embarrassingly, she ran out of the ability to finish her sentence.

Lifting a wry eyebrow, Hal sighed. It didn't help Kit's case that the gesture made him look irresistibly endearing…almost boyish.

'What you've said is true,' he said. 'But in the past couple of days I've developed feelings for you that go beyond just wanting you to work for me and they won't go away. I may have a broken leg, but that doesn't stop me from having the same needs as any other able-bodied red-blooded man.'

Curling her hair behind her ear, Kit knew it was a delaying tactic, but still she asked softly, 'Exactly what kind of needs are we talking about?'

'Scoot up next to me and I'll tell you. Better still, I'll demonstrate.'

'No.'

'Come on. I dare you. I want to try an experiment.'

She wanted to say something…*anything*. But forming words seemed impossible when her mouth had suddenly gone dry as sand and her tongue didn't respond in tandem with her brain. Hal Treverne had put her in a dizzying spin and it wasn't a state she was familiar with. She'd frequently anguished about her mother not having any common sense when it came to men, but where was hers now, when she needed it? Perhaps more than she'd ever needed it before?

Moistening her suddenly dry lips with her tongue, she made herself ask, 'What kind of experiment are you talking about?'

Hal's glance was unwaveringly direct.

'I want to kiss you, Katherine with a K. *Properly* this time. And I want you to kiss me back. If neither of us enjoy the experience then there's no harm done. We'll simply carry on as before. I want to reassure you that there's no danger of your job being jeopardised. I give you my word on that. You'll stay until our arrangement naturally comes to an end—when I'm completely mobile again. Agreed?'

The silence that followed this inflammatory statement was deafening.

Hal was gesturing for Kit to move closer, and when she gazed back into his eyes the sight was akin to gazing into a mirage of mesmerising crystal waters after she'd stumbled through a burning hot desert without hope of ever having a drink again.

How could she possibly ignore the chance that her

mirage might turn out to be a genuine vision and that it would save her life if she drank from it?

She reached out her hand to slide it over Hal's. His skin was silkily smooth and warm, as it always was. But this time she had permission to actively *enjoy* the experience—not just tend to his practical needs as she normally did.

With a heated, lazy smile he tugged her hand to bring her close into his side. Before Kit even had time to gasp he'd pushed aside the heavy fall of her hair and laid his palm against her nape. *Everything tingled.* Then he hungrily drew her head towards his. Any opportunity or desire for further conversation disappeared abruptly the instant he touched his lips to hers. The texture of them was like the most seductive velvet and they tasted like nectar.

When Hal's tongue dived into her mouth and duelled with hers pleasure such as she'd never known before suffused her—a delight so intensely hot and sensual that it was like a tropical storm descending out of a summer sky. Its sudden surprising appearance gave her no chance to find shelter. The only thing she could do was surrender, give herself up to its fierce elemental nature with no thought or concern of where the experience might lead her. *Was she brave enough to do that?* The more Hal kissed her, the more she wanted to fly into the face of her fear and challenge it.

Then he cupped her breast through her sweater, evoking a ravenous need in her blood that made her feel as if she was losing her mind with no hope of ever thinking straight again…like someone standing too close to a crumbling cliff-edge and dangerously being compelled to jump. Why did she suddenly feel that she would willingly sacrifice her dream of a safe place, a bolthole she could call her own, to travel into the unknown with him?

With a helpless whimper Kit anchored her hands round Hal's iron-hard biceps, her fingers gripping hard, wishing she had the courage to lift up his sweater so that she might touch him more intimately and press her body into his.

Hal's head and heart were reeling. He knew what it was like occasionally to drink more than one generous glass of intoxicating red wine at dinner, to have his head spin and his limbs turn to water, but never before had he experienced sensations as dizzyingly seductive and addictive as this! Kit's ravishing mouth and silken tongue were so sinfully delicious that he knew he could willingly be a slave to her kisses for a very long time indeed, whilst her *body*... Her body and her scent aroused him more than any other woman's had ever aroused him before.

The need to take this so-called experiment further was growing more and more demanding. He was so hot and hard that he had to tear his lips away from Kit's to take a steadying breath and try to calm his escalating need. As he moved his hands up to cup her face Hal's breath felt no less steady as he stared hungrily down into the incandescent blue eyes that gazed back at him. They looked as stunned and as intoxicated as he was.

'I want to take you to bed, Kit.' With a wry smile he added, 'Let me rephrase that. I *need* to take you to bed. Our little experiment was more...much more successful than I'd hoped it would be.'

To his surprise, Kit responded with a troubled sigh.

'We can't always have what we want or—or need,

Hal…and perhaps giving in to our base desires isn't the best thing to do for either of us. I won't deny that I find you attractive, but if you seriously think about this you'll know it isn't a good idea to take things any further. We've already crossed a boundary I vowed never to cross with a client. You've been hurt in an accident and forced to take a much slower pace than you're used to while you recuperate, and I've been hired to help you.'

Reaching up, she gently freed his hands from round her face and sat back against the couch's sumptuous leather upholstery, a shapely leg tucked beneath her.

'It's understandable that you're feeling frustrated and lonely, but I'm not the cure for either of those states— even though you might think I am.' Visibly blushing she added, 'Your kiss was lovely, and so are you. But I'd rather you remembered me as a reliable and competent help when you most needed it than some convenient woman you took to bed simply because you were feeling horny.'

As shocked surprise eddied through him Hal hardly knew what to say. Kit had told him he was 'lovely' and yet she clearly didn't trust his motives. A thought that might explain why she was so uneasy about taking things further suddenly struck him.

'You think I'm just the same as one of those low-lifes who used your mother then abandoned her. That's it, isn't it?' He cursed out loud because he knew it was true.

'No. Of course I don't think that!' Her mouth shaping a painful grimace, Kit folded her arms over her chest and dipped her head. The sudden movement caused her glorious hair to tumble forward onto her shoulders in a riot of silken burnished waves.

Hal sucked in a breath. The sight was so beautiful…

'I know you're not like them,' she declared. 'But I have to protect myself. There's no one else looking out for me but *me*. I've got a reputation for being competent and reliable at the agency and I need a good reference when I leave you if I'm to get another job as good as this. Don't you understand?'

Starting to feel a little calmer, Hal was thoughtful. 'I've given you my word that you won't lose this job, and if you see it through to the end of course I'll give you a good reference…the *best*. I want to reassure you about that. But I can't pretend it's going to make me want you any less, Kit, or that you'll stop thinking about that kiss we just shared.'

'Okay.' She smiled, but it was plain to see her expression was still guarded. 'I'm flattered that you want me—I really am. I know that you could probably just pick up the phone and have any woman that you want. And I'm sorry if I offended you with what I said about you being—'

'Horny?' he finished helpfully.

'Sometimes I'm a little too quick to speak my mind.'

'Do you think I don't know that by now?'

'Anyway…' Uncurling her leg from beneath her, Kit ran her hand over her hair, as if to tidy it, then positioned herself more comfortably against the cushions. 'Why don't we just finish watching the film? I was really starting to enjoy it.'

Hal's strongly defined jaw clenched ruefully. 'There's something else I'd much rather do, but seeing as I'm a gentleman this time I'll give you the prerogative of choosing the evening's entertainment. Next time it will be *my* turn.'

MAGGIE COX   101

'If you're no longer so keen on watching the film perhaps you might like a game of chess instead?' The look she gave him was innocence personified. 'But if we play I warn you I'm no push-over. I don't take any prisoners. I play to win!'

His blood heated again, painfully reminding him of what he'd given up in deference to reassuring Kit that he was no ruthless playboy who believed it was his God-given right to take what he wanted. Lowering his voice, he remarked, 'So do I, sweetheart. I don't see the point of playing a game if I don't come out on top. After all, being on top is what I do best.'

Hal couldn't deny the sense of satisfaction that pulsed through him when her pretty cheeks turned revealingly pink...

Over the next few days Hal played the part of the gentleman he professed to be to the max. Gone was the teasing, provocative banter that Kit had come to love and expect, that suggested he was more bad boy than gentleman. A much more sedate, thoughtful man took his place. In fact he'd become so quiet that she fretted his leg wasn't healing as well as it should be and that it was seriously bothering him. When she checked with him he always immediately denied anything was amiss and returned to the book he was reading, or to his study to work, with an expression that told her friendly conversation was off the agenda and he would prefer not to be disturbed.

There was no more talk of him choosing their nightly entertainment either. Kit couldn't deny she wasn't upset about that. *Her nightly dreams were all about Hal.* So much so that she sometimes woke up in a sweat, with her heart racing dizzyingly. Her visions of him and her together were so real that she was crushed when she woke up and realised they were just nocturnal fantasies. She might get to the end of this job with her self-enforced celibacy intact, but that didn't mean she would be remotely happy about it—not when her heart already ached at the mere idea of parting from Hal for good.

When the nurse paid her next visit to examine his injured leg and with a cheerful smile declared it to be 'healing nicely', adding that it was just a matter of time before he would return to full strength, to Kit's mind Hal didn't seem entirely convinced. When the nurse went on to say that he should take advantage of some regular physiotherapy before seeing his consultant again, and that Kit should make sure to keep up the RICE treatment, he gave a brief nod of agreement, thanked her for the advice and saw her to the door in his wheelchair.

He still wasn't in the mood for conversation, it seemed...

The night after the nurse's visit Kit lay in bed, staring up at the shadowed ceiling in her bedroom for what seemed like hours, because she'd been alternately teased and tormented by the memory of Hal's taste in her mouth and his hands on her body and as a result sleep evaded her. But eventually she fell into a fitful doze.

A loud shout woke her up. Immediately responding, she hurriedly pushed aside the sheets and counterpane and scrambled to her feet. Without even pausing to grab the striped cotton robe she'd draped over the back of a slipper chair, she ran outside into the corridor and pushed opened Hal's bedroom door.

The soft light in the hallway more than adequately

illuminated the room. Wearing navy silk boxers, Hal was positioned half in and half out of the voluminous bed, gripping onto the oyster-coloured silk sheets for grim death as his cast-covered leg precariously slid towards the floor.

Kit grabbed hold of him to prevent him from falling just in the nick of time. His broad, hard-muscled back was slippery with sweat and it was no easy feat to lift and push his heavy masculine frame safely back onto the bed, because he was clearly still half asleep and in no position to help her. Thankfully her reaction had been lightning-quick and had saved the day. A heavy fall onto that broken bone of his would have set him back several months at least, she was sure.

As he fell back against the pillows and stared dazedly up at her she gently ran her hand over his forehead, pushing back the rebellious dark curls that brushed against it.

'Are you okay? You gave me an almighty shock when I heard you cry out like that.'

'I'm fine.' Although Hal's smile was definitely on the drowsy side, his mercurial hazel eyes still managed a mischievous twinkle. 'Thanks to you. You really are my guardian angel, aren't you, Kit? Quite apt that you should rescue me when I was dreaming that you were in my arms.'

Still leaning over him, Kit turned as still as a statue. The remark had sent her own temperature skyrocketing and she was suddenly aware that the only thing separating them was the flimsy chemise she wore, which she'd impulsively bought from a vintage market stall in the Portobello Road. In truth, it was totally impractical, but she loved it. With its spaghetti shoulder straps, and a scooped neckline that just about covered her breasts, it was probably the most feminine item of clothing she possessed. And beneath the hyacinth-coloured material, apart from her panties, she was as bare as the day she was born.

'It must have been quite a dream if it nearly made you fall out of bed,' she replied huskily.

'It was. If it was graded by a panel of judges, the medal it would win would definitely be gold.'

'What were you doing…? *Wrestling* with me?'

Hal's chameleon golden-eyed gaze was no longer drowsy but wide and alert. In a flash his hands moved to fasten themselves round Kit's slender-boned wrists and her heart thudded so hard in surprise that the desire to be free again didn't even cross her mind.

'I was passionately making love to you, and I guess we both got a little carried away.' He smiled teasingly.

Riveted, Kit stared. 'Well…'

His indisputably aroused gaze was roaming over the curves of her creamy breasts in the body-skimming nightwear and she was only too aware that his own magnificent bare chest was mere tantalising inches away from hers,

'I'd advise you to try and have less, shall we say… *energetic* dreams in future. Especially when they could potentially endanger your health.'

'What if I think the dream was worth the potential danger? I'm not a man who plays safe. I like to take risks, remember?'

His well-shaped lips formed a slow, seductive smile and the heat from his body mingled with his arresting cologne and made Kit feel seriously weak. As she stared back into his chiselled handsome face any desire to do the sensible thing and free herself completely deserted her.

'I know,' she answered softly. 'It's what you're famous for, isn't it? Taking risks, I mean. But seriously, Hal, I've been so worried. You've hardly spoken a word to me over the past few days. Is there something wrong that you're not telling me about?'

'No, sweetheart. There's nothing bothering me other than frustration at so stupidly injuring myself and not being able to take control of things as I usually do.'

Kit breathed out a relieved sigh. 'Is that all? Don't you know those feelings aren't a permanent state? Bones heal and your frustration will fade just as soon as you're up and about again, like you were before. In no time at all this setback will be nothing but a distant memory. I promise.'

'Hmm, you're probably right. But, talking of another kind of frustration, did I tell you how sexy I think that little number you're *almost* wearing is?' he murmured, deftly pushing aside the inadequate spaghetti straps so that they slid down over her slim arms and caused the bodice of her chemise to reveal even more of her. 'Do you have *any* idea how beautiful you are?' he husked, his darkened gaze avidly roaming her now almost completely exposed bare breasts.

The cool night air that drifted in from the partially opened window skimmed her nipples and hardened them to prickling, tight steel buds. But Kit knew in truth it wasn't anything external that made her react physically like that. It was her desire and hunger for Hal, and its force was like a torrid drowning wave she couldn't do anything but surrender to.

'I want to make love to you, Kit. Will you let me?'

'What about—what about your injured leg? I don't want to risk hurting you.'

For answer he put his fingers across her lips to quieten her. 'I'm sure that between us we can find a position where there'll be no risk to my leg. Let's work it out, shall we? It will be an adventure.' His compelling eyes darkened even more. 'Are you in the mood for an adventure, Kit? I'm hoping that the answer is yes.'

Before she could utter a word Hal's hands were driving through her hair, pulling her down on top of him and searing her lips with urgent scalding kisses that made her gasp and moan for more. She was all but on fire for him. The temperature of her blood surely couldn't be far from reaching boiling point, and she didn't resist when he guided her carefully over him so that she was sitting astride his toned, fit body.

As she settled herself straight away Kit became intimately aware of the steely hardness beneath the sensuous silk of his shorts, but she didn't encourage or succumb to inviting his possession straight away, no matter how eager she felt. She didn't just want to *receive* pleasure; she wanted to *give* it too. Sitting back for a moment to observe him, she knew her appreciative smile couldn't help but be seductive. Henry Treverne was one of the most beautiful men she had ever seen, and she wanted to make the most of her time with him—however long or short that might turn out to be.

With a soft sigh Kit bent her head again. But instead of meeting his lips she slowly licked down his chest, from his flat male nipples to the column of dark silky hair that disappeared into his boxers.

CHAPTER EIGHT

'Do you know what you're doing to me, woman?' Hal growled as Kit teased and taunted him by swirling her indescribably silky tongue round his nipples, then slowly and deliberately sweeping it down to his navel.

Her blue eyes twinkling, she lifted her head and gave him the most maddeningly innocent smile. 'I like to think I'm doing something nice. Don't you like it?'

'Of course I like it! But I want you to come back up here so that I can do the same to you.'

'All right, then. Your wish is my command.'

'Don't say that or you may find I have a veritable list of wishes that will keep you here for the rest of the night and most of tomorrow too. What do you think about that?'

'I'm beginning to see that you have a very creative mind, Mr Treverne. But if I don't agree with any of your requests I'll simply make myself scarce and go back to bed.'

She made this declaration as she rose to face him, and it took every ounce of will Hal possessed to suppress a heartfelt groan at the arresting sight she made. With her fiery copper hair tumbling onto her bared rosy-tipped breasts Kit reminded him of the eponymous

Moll Flanders from the classic Defoe novel. As well as being bewitchingly beautiful, everything about her was irresistibly sexy. He'd defy any red-blooded male not to want to possess her.

Reaching out his hands to cup her breasts, he luxuriated in the soft weight and satiny feel of them as he stroked and teased the rigid nipples. Then, unable to deny his growing need to know her more intimately, he captured one of them between his lips and suckled and laved until she cried out and her head fell forward onto his chest. It was apparent that his lover had experienced a spontaneous release, and Hal couldn't deny the sense of privilege that made him feel…that he could do that for her.

He was gratified that she was so exquisitely sensitive. *Had she been as sensitive as this with any other of the lovers she'd had in the past?* The thought struck a discordant jealous note that briefly unsettled him. But he refused to let it taint his pleasure for long.

With a smile, he tenderly smoothed his hand down over the tumbling red-gold curls that nestled just beneath his chin. When Kit tipped up her head to glance at him her cheeks had the bloom of a ripe red apple and her blue-eyed glance appeared surprisingly guilty.

'I—I don't know what to say…'

'Did you enjoy it?'

She blushed again. 'Yes, I did.'

'Well, there's no need to feel guilty if you enjoyed it, is there? I don't want either of us to have any regrets about being together like this. In truth, the attraction we feel for each other has been building up for a while— you know that. And I don't want you to feel guilty just because you experienced pleasure. Trust me, there's going to be plenty more of that coming your way. We haven't finished yet. Not by a long chalk. But first...' he jerked his head towards the satinwood cabinet next to the bed '...I think I'm going to need to use some protection—that's unless you're already covered?'

Sliding carefully to the side of the bed, Kit sat up, her hands immediately adjusting the thin straps of her chemise back over her shoulders and tugging the bodice up higher to cover her breasts.

'I'm not on the pill, if that's what you mean. There's been no need. Just in case you want to know, I haven't had sex in a very long time.'

Hal's heart missed a beat. 'How long?'

She frowned. 'The last time...and the *first* time, in fact—was when I was seduced by a man who turned out to be married. It only happened the once.' Her shoulders lifted in a pained shrug. 'It was a stupid mistake that I deeply regret. I'm just thankful that I had the common sense to make sure he used protection.'

For a moment Hal didn't know what to say. When he finally managed to make sense of his feelings, he asked, 'And when did this happen?'

'I'd just turned twenty-one and had gone to a club with some friends. That's where I met him. Anyway, like I said, it was a long time ago.'

'And since then you've really never been with anyone else?'

'No.'

'Why not?'

'Do you really need to ask? Don't you think I'd be wary of men after what happened? Being deceived like that made me feel dirty. I never want to experience such a feeling again, and it made me more aware than ever that relationships shouldn't be a priority—that I should just focus on trying to make a better life for myself. That was and still *is* my main priority. Shall I get the protection for you?'

With a slightly bemused nod of his dark head Hal indicated his agreement even as he resolved to delve a little deeper into her surprising confession at the earliest opportunity—to find out a bit more about the cheating rat who had stolen her virginity and deceived her.

'You'll find some in the second drawer down.'

As soon as Kit had handed the foil packet over to him he wasted no time in pulling her back against his chest and passionately claiming her lips in a languorous open-mouthed kiss. As he did so he tugged down the straps of her chemise until he was satisfied he could feel her lovely breasts again. Then, still kissing her, he shaped his hands over her pretty bottom and started to ease her panties down over her svelte hips as much as he could manage without jeopardising his injured leg.

Although he was more than ready to take her, and almost in pain because his desire was so acute, Hal didn't want to rush anything, so he made sure to take his time exploring his lover's supple and slender body. *It was hardly a sacrifice…* Not when her skin was as soft as down and as satiny-smooth as the finest silk. And, being that her only experience of lovemaking had been with a man who had lied to her about being free so that he could get what he wanted from her, Hal's greatest desire was to make this experience with him one Kit would *never* forget—but only for the best of reasons. He wasn't promising her something he couldn't deliver, but he honestly wanted to help her erase that painful episode from her mind and replace it with a much better one.

Earlier Hal had joked that he liked to be on top, but because of his injury it was only natural that Kit should straddle him, and with her surprisingly strong slender thighs clasping him, and her tumbled copper hair and bare tip-tilted breasts on seductive view for his personal pleasure and edification, he had no qualms in silently admitting that, in truth, he actually had the best position of all...

With his hands settling either side of her womanly hips, Hal suddenly couldn't wait any longer to fulfil his growing need for her—and told her so. 'If I don't take you now, angel, I might—just *might*—lose my mind. But you'll have to help me take these boxers off.' When she'd accomplished the task he told her, 'Now it's your turn.'

With the same graceful and athletic prowess she'd used to remove his boxers, and mindful again not to jar the cast on his leg, Kit reached down and carefully slid her flimsy underwear down to her ankles. Then she scrunched the delicate cotton into a ball and threw it onto the floor.

When she resumed her position, Hal murmured huskily, 'You were gone too long, baby.' Hungrily fastening his hands either side of her flushed face, beneath the bewitching cascade of her burnished copper hair, he finished, 'I missed you.'

'I missed you too.' She bent down teasingly to brush her fulsome moist lips against his mouth, making him groan.

Before he could completely surrender to his burning desire he ripped open the silver foil packet he still held in his closed fist and fitted the latex protection over his member. *He was rock-hard.* The soft gasp Kit couldn't prevent feathered over him. Reaching for her once again, Hal knew it wouldn't be easy for him to be as mindful of her inexperience as he would like to be, and as much as she deserved, and he honestly regretted that. But his hunger for this woman was off the scale...

Never before in his history of conquests had it been this wanton or voracious. When he placed the tip of his member at her moist entrance and pushed upwards without preamble her satin heat all but overwhelmed him. He had no choice but to take things slowly or his love-making would be over almost as soon as it had begun.

Any tension Kit might have felt at the thought of properly uniting her body with a man's after five long years of sexual abstinence quickly disappeared the moment Hal's hard silken manhood entered her body. *It was as though she'd been waiting all this time just for him.* Although her feminine muscles might be understandably tight due to her inexperience, Hal's initial thrust had not been as painful or shockingly invasive as she'd expected. In fact after a brief searing sting his possession hardly made her flinch at all it was so natural. And the fact didn't detract from the inconceivable pleasure that filled her.

It was like drowning in a sea of the most exquisite honey. She'd honestly never felt more alive or glad to be a woman as she did right then. And as he drove into her again and again, and she allowed herself to relax completely, she didn't have the slightest reticence about meeting his voracious hunger with her own, bending her head greedily to kiss the side of his chiselled jaw and forehead and nip the velvet lobe of his ear.

How was it possible that a man's body could taste this good or feel so wonderful? she mused. It made her wonder how she'd survived so long without such sublime intimacy and gratification. The heat that filled her made her feel as though her blood was being lit by a fire. A fire whose flames took a sudden fierce hold to lick higher and higher. In fact it grew so hot that when Hal clasped her head between his hands to kiss her more deeply it couldn't help but ignite sparks and reach a crescendo.

She already knew she was sensitive to his touch—that had been highlighted by her spontaneous climax when he'd kissed her breasts earlier. Now, as Kit gasped her pleasure into his mouth, the sensation that poured through her was akin to riding a wave whose natural destiny was to join the falls that plunged over a cliff edge into a crystal-clear sun-kissed ocean. It was the most exhilarating ride she had ever experienced, and it was everything she'd dreamed it would be. Her heart had never beaten so hard or so fast with excitement.

Even as she stilled breathlessly Hal held her tightly against him. Once more his narrow athletic hips rocked against her smooth inner thighs and his rhythmic thrusts grew deeper and more purposeful. The helpless shout he released as his desire reached its peak echoed round the room. Apart from their preoccupied presence the air was almost preternaturally still. Just as if it had been waiting for their breathless sighs of pleasure and satisfaction to fill it.

Seeing a muscle in the side of her lover's lean, carved face suddenly flinch, Kit eased herself up, her heartbeat accelerating for an entirely different reason.

'Are you all right? Have I leant too hard on your leg and hurt it? Tell me, Hal…I need to know.'

Even as she carefully disengaged her body from his and moved to lie next to him he straight away hauled her back against his chest and drove his hands through her hair.

'Stop worrying about me and let me tell you how amazing that was—how utterly delicious and gorgeous you are.'

'It's my job to be concerned about you, Hal.'

He raised a lightly mocking eyebrow. 'Does that mean you wouldn't worry about me unless you were being paid to?'

A mortifying wave of heat assailed her. In her mind Kit couldn't help privately cursing her inability to relax right then and say what she really wanted to say—that she cared for him more than she'd ever cared for anyone before and that it scared her, that she hated the idea of him being in pain and wished that it was somehow in her power to spare him the hurt.

'Of course it doesn't. When I saw you wince then I was just concerned that we might have put too much strain on your femur and maybe damaged it even more.'

With a soft chuckle Hal slid his hand beneath her delicate jaw and gazed deeply into her eyes. 'Don't you know that what we just did helped me feel the best that I've felt in a very long time? I mean it. Not just because it was great sex…and it *was*…but because you're a genuinely compassionate and caring woman and I'm so pleased that I've met you, Kit.'

She'd never been remotely easy with receiving compliments and now she found out that it was even harder receiving them from Hal. It was hard because it really mattered to have his good opinion.

'Thank you. It's very sweet of you to say so.'

His lips hitched in a rueful grimace. 'Sweet? I can honestly say that no-one's ever accused me of being *that* before.'

'Not even your mother when you were a little boy?'

In a flash his expression darkened. 'My mother left when Sam and I were kids. I have no memory of her ever calling me anything endearing or anything else, for that matter. Shall we change the subject?'

Kit was mortified that she'd inadvertently hurt him with her remark. 'I'm sorry I said that. I didn't know.'

Taking a deep breath in, Hal sighed, 'Of course you didn't—how could you? And how could I possibly be offended because you've stumbled on a subject that you weren't even aware might be awkward for me?' His gaze was distant and reflective for a moment, but it wasn't long before he returned his attention to Kit and smiled. 'One day I might tell you a bit more about my tale of woe, but not right now.' His strong arms encircled her waist. 'The only thing I want to do right now is hold you and breathe you in. I love that scent you're wearing…what's it called? It smells very natural.'

'It *is* natural. It's just me. I've never had any cause to wear scent to bed.'

'And you don't have one now, sweetheart. I love the fact that the alluring perfume I can detect on your skin is purely your own natural scent. You know what? I want to fall asleep with you beside me tonight, Kit. Will you stay with me until the morning? If it's any incentive, I promise you I don't snore.'

'Even if you did I'd probably just grin and bear it because you're so hunky,' she teased.

'You think so?'

Beneath his shadowed complexion she saw him colour.

'I confess it's not the first time I've been called that. The tabloids use the word with monotonous regularity to describe me when they're spouting some spurious story about some model or soap starlet they want to portray as being linked with me. It gets a little tiresome, to tell you the truth. The phrase "Hunky Hal Treverne" makes me feel more like a stereotype than a person. Although I have to say the description sounds much more complimentary coming from *you*, sweetheart.'

'Oh...' Kit couldn't help feeling a little defensive at his comment that the tabloid press used the word with 'monotonous regularity'. Did he think that was where she had got it from? If he did, then it didn't suggest she had much discernment.

It hit a particularly sensitive nerve to be inadvertently reminded that she wasn't as well-educated as a lot of women her age, who'd perhaps gone on to university when they'd left school. *In truth, it was one of the big regrets of her life.* As for reading the tabloids—she didn't give them the time of day. She'd probably seen the more salacious headlines about Hal on the internet...not because she'd deliberately sought them out but because along with other celebrity gossip they'd flashed up on the site she used to check her e-mail from time to time.

But his comment also reminded her that not only was he an educated man himself but also the son of landed gentry, and suddenly the jolting realisation made Kit's heart sink like a stone. If their lovemaking had lulled her even for a second into believing the improbable fantasy that they might go on to enjoy a *real* relationship then she'd best dissuade herself of such an idea as quickly as possible. Hadn't she promised herself she'd never go down the same soulless destructive path with men as her mother had? *She'd already made one unfortunate mistake in trusting a man.*

Hal Treverne was destined to marry a woman from his own privileged class—not someone like Kit, just an ordinary working class girl, whose father had been a Romany gypsy who had abandoned her mother when he'd found out she was pregnant. Sooner or later Hal would wake up to the fact she wasn't in his league and no doubt regret bedding her. The thought that he wouldn't think that their intimacy was anything special as time went by almost made her want to *weep*.

Because she'd suddenly fallen silent, Hal looked concerned. The softly diffused lighting streaming in through the partially opened door highlighted his compelling gaze, made his irises glint like gold.

'What's wrong? You've suddenly gone quiet on me.'

As she tried to tidy the now crumpled silk chemise so that it covered her a bit more, Kit's smile was tremulous. 'I don't think I *will* spend the night with you, if you don't mind? I need to be up early to see to a few things…'

'What things are those?'

'Well, I—I need to make a shopping list, and also figure out menus for the day.'

'If that means you can't spend the night with me then we'll simply order in some food instead. Didn't my sister tell you that your main priority should be meeting my needs?'

'You *are* the priority…of course you are…but—'

'I don't like the sound of that "but",' Hal commented, sounding a bit more than vaguely irritated. 'Go on.'

'It probably wasn't a very good idea…us getting together like, this I mean.'

'Are you saying that you regret it?' Now his expression was seriously perturbed.

She coloured a little. 'Not the experience—no. It's just that—well, it could make our day-to-day relationship rather awkward. It's still going to be quite a while before you can get around completely unaided and, like you said, your needs have to take priority. Anything that detracts from that wouldn't be good. Perhaps it might be best if you contacted the agency and asked for someone else to come in and help you? Someone more impartial than I'm able to be now.'

'Stop it. Stop this nonsense right this minute.'

The scowl on his handsome face was nothing less than formidable, and Kit's pulse skittered in alarm.

'I promised you that whatever happened between us it wouldn't jeopardise your job, and I meant it. If you think I've changed my mind then you're crazy. Just because I desire you it doesn't mean that I don't need your help any more. And I don't want someone else from the damn agency. All I want is you.'

'That's all well and good, Hal, but I'm just trying to think of what's best for you. Can't you see that?'

'And what about *you*, Kit? Do you really think it's best for you that you leave me high and dry with no new job lined up, after you've promised to stay with me at least until I'm mobile again?'

Hearing the sincerity in Hal's tone, along with the fear that she might just up and leave him, Kit couldn't deny her relief that he wanted her to stay. He was right—she'd made him a promise. And, no, she *didn't* have another job lined up, and it *would* hurt her just as much as it would hurt him to walk out now.

Knowing she should stay if she wanted to preserve her hard-won reputation with the agency and secure another job afterwards, she resigned herself to doing just that.

As far as her relationship with Hal was concerned she wouldn't expect anything more from him other than his thanks and respect when her job here was done, and as long as she had that, given time, she would get over this heartfelt attraction for him. If she was going to live the dependable and comfortable existence that she longed for and buy herself that little bolthole she'd been so diligently saving for, then the sooner she got over him the better she would be for it.

'Okay. No doubt you're right. I *would* be letting myself down if I didn't see the job through—although I am disappointed in myself because I broke a cast-iron rule not to get personally involved with a client. If I'm to continue to do my job well, Hal, I can't risk a repeat of what happened between us tonight. You know, I can't.'

CHAPTER NINE

HAL STARED AT Kit in disbelief. Did she really think to draw a line under what they had just shared as if it had never happened? It looked as if she *did*. She was already getting out of bed and turning her back on him, her hands tugging down her pretty silk chemise as if to hide herself—almost as if she was ashamed of succumbing to their passionate union. He couldn't bear the thought that the only reason she'd agreed to stay was to fulfil her contract with the agency, not because of any personal regard for him...

Manoeuvring himself upright, he ground out, 'Did I delude myself that what we just shared meant something to you, Kit? I mean, other than just fulfilling a very basic need?'

She turned her head at that, and her oval face was as pale as a winter moon even in the dimmed light that streamed in from the corridor.

'I'm not saying it didn't mean anything. I'm just saying that it can't happen again. You must know it can't. I'm a realist, if nothing else, and this impetuous turning in the road that we've suddenly taken can only lead to a dead-end. When you're back on your feet again you'll realise that and be glad that we didn't take it any further.'

'Will I? You know that for a fact, do you?'

Her eyes were downcast for a moment. Then, as if garnering more determination to stick to her decision, Kit lifted her head. 'Now, tell me—do you need anything before I go back to my room? I can help you into the bathroom, if you'd like?'

'So you intend to play the coolly professional nurse from now on rather than my lover?' Hal found it hard to prevent the anger and resentment that seeped into his tone. 'I know which one I prefer, and it isn't the nurse.'

Her lovely blue eyes reflected her anguish at his stinging remark.

'My intention is to fulfil my obligation to both you and the agency.' Her restless twisting hands confirmed that his words had hurt her. 'I won't say any more than that. I'd better let you rest. I'm very tired and I need to get some sleep. You must be tired too, so I'll say goodnight.'

She stooped to collect the scrunched-up underwear she'd disposed of earlier, when Hal had enticed her into bed, and as he watched her Hal's resentment curdled like bitter aloes in the pit of his stomach. *He was so sick of being abandoned.* It was becoming a soul-destroying pattern in his life. It had started with his mother, and then his father, who—no matter what Hal achieved or did—would never be proud of him. He hadn't even been able to put his cynical judgement of his son aside to visit him in the hospital when he'd been injured. *And now Kit—the woman he found himself more attracted to than any other—was turning her back on him...*

Gritting his teeth and shoving his hair back from his

forehead, he said scathingly, 'I'll be sure to call on you if I need anything. I'd keep your door open, if I were you…just in case you don't hear me should I call out your name. It wouldn't bode well for your exemplary record at the agency if I were to fall out of bed again and injure myself, would it?'

Her cheeks reddening, Kit said quietly, 'I would never let anything like that happen to you. You have my word on that. And it's not just about protecting my record with the agency. I—I care about what happens to you.'

'Do you really?'

'Yes, I do. Anyway, I'll make sure to keep my door ajar so I can hear you, should you need me.'

'I need you *now*, but you don't seem to care about that. If you did then you'd stay the night with me as I asked.'

Hal caught a glimpse of what looked like regret in her bewitching blue eyes and for a moment his heart leapt with hope that she might change her mind. But instead she gracefully moved across to the door and went out, making sure to leave it slightly ajar instead of shutting it completely.

'Damn and blast it all to hell!' Dropping back down against his pillows, he freely gave vent to his anger and frustration…

He'd had the most diabolical night's sleep—perhaps an hour or two at most. So when he wheeled himself into the kitchen the next morning in search of Kit and a cup of much-needed coffee Hal wasn't exactly predisposed to be either amenable or pleasant.

Nor was he easily going to forgive her for not accepting his invitation to spend the night with him—even though he'd reflected afterwards that it was probably a good thing that she hadn't. After all, his romantic interludes had always been on *his* terms, not his lover's, and that was the way he liked it. Certainly he had never invited any of his partners to spend the night with him before. It shouldn't be any different with Kit—no matter *how* much he desired her. Nor should he behave as if it remotely disturbed him that she'd refused his invitation to stay the night. If she intuited that he needed her more than he let on then that would make him vulnerable, and that was the one thing he wanted to avoid...

Usually when something was troubling him Hal's habit was to take some exercise—either to jog, run or take a bike-ride—so that he could think what to do. Because all of those outlets were denied him right now the sensation that the walls of his surroundings were pressing in on him added to the already considerable stress he was under. He longed to get out—to fill his lungs with some fresh air and breathe freely again.

Kit was standing by the worktop waiting for the kettle to boil when he entered. Her beautiful red hair had been curtailed into two neat plaits, and dressed in jeans and a tunic-style white shirt—wearing no make-up as far as he could tell—she looked just like a schoolgirl. Despite his irritability, Hal's heart missed a beat. He might be mad at her for running out on him last night, but it didn't make him want her any less. The blood in his veins was already simmering at the mere sight of her, and the thought that he might never again have her in his bed soured his already dark mood even more.

'Morning,' he muttered, deliberately averting his gaze and wheeling himself across to the table.

'I was just about to bring you in some coffee and toast and help you to get dressed.' She stopped speaking and sighed, and Hal couldn't resist lifting his head to check out her expression. 'But I see you've managed it without me,' she finished.

'I'm not entirely helpless,' he returned gruffly. To his astonishment, her lips curved in an amused smile—which wasn't the reaction he'd expected. 'What's so funny?' he demanded, privately furious that she might be mocking him.

The smile vanished. 'You've put your sweater on back to front.'

Glancing downwards, Hal saw that she was right. The grey cashmere V-neck was indeed back to front. Hardly welcoming the fact being pointed out to him, he muttered a curse and then impatiently pulled it up over his head. Bare-chested, it didn't help to maintain his dignity when he got into a tussle with one of the sleeves in an attempt to turn the sweater the right way round so he that could put it back on again.

Kit instantly reacted. 'Let me help you.'

Presenting herself in front of him, she carefully relieved Hal of the cashmere, sorted it out so he could put it back on, and gently pulled the jumper down over his head. By the time she'd completed the task, tugging it gently but firmly down to his hard lean waist as though he were a child, his heart was thudding fit to burst. It didn't help matters that he found it almost unbearable to be so close to her and not be able to spontaneously reach out, pull her down onto his lap and embrace her.

'For God's sake, stop fussing, woman! How old do you think I am? *Three?* If you want something useful to do you can go and see to my coffee and toast.'

'I intend to do just that,' she answered primly, her hands crossed over her chest. 'But a simple thank you for helping you out wouldn't go amiss. My mother may not have been an educated woman, or have been able to afford for me to stay on at school, but the one thing she absolutely insisted on when she raised me was my having good manners. I think manners can tell you a lot about a person.'

The revealing comment stopped Hal from coming back at her with a cutting or flippant rejoinder. He frowned. 'Does it bother you that you had to leave school early and didn't get a better education?'

At first she turned away from him. But she turned back again almost immediately, her hands on her hips and her cheeks flushed. 'It depends what you mean by "a better education". I may not have been to college or university, or studied for a profession, but I'm not stupid. I've learned a lot on my way to becoming a fully-fledged adult—including the wisdom to know what's best for me and the importance of making good decisions. I've learned that you suffer if you don't. There are a lot of important facts about life that even a privileged or expensive education can't buy, you know.'

'Are you perhaps suggesting that my own education was privileged and expensive?'

The rosy tint on Kit's alabaster cheeks grew even pinker. 'It's pretty well documented that it was. Are you saying that's not true?'

'It's true. I did indeed have a privileged and expensive education. I also grew up with the proverbial silver spoon in my mouth. But does that make me a bad person? A person you wouldn't think it worthwhile getting to know? I may have had most of the material advantages that a lot of people aspire to having, but that doesn't protect a person from experiencing the challenges we all have to face as humans and nor should it.'

To his surprise Hal's heart was racing as he came to the end of his little speech, and he realised just how much resentment and hurt he'd harboured over the years at being perceived as 'having it all'—meaning he couldn't possibly understand what it was like to go without anything and therefore his opinion shouldn't count. *That just wasn't true.* He *did* know what it was like to go without. The most fundamental thing a human being needed in life was to know that he was loved, Hal believed. But aside from the love of his sister Sam that was the commodity that he had been bereft of most of all.

'You said—you said that you'd tell me more about your mother leaving. Was that one of the challenges you meant?'

It was extraordinary how Kit seemed to have the unerring ability to get straight to the heart of something, he thought. Rubbing his hand round his jaw, Hal shook his head. 'I don't want to talk about that. Maybe if you'd consented to spending the night with me I might have told you. But all I want right now is my breakfast, and after that I just want to get out of here for a while.'

'I'm sorry that you no longer want to tell me about your past…about your mother I mean. But I understand why you don't. You think that I let you down by not agreeing to stay with you last night. Maybe you even think it was easy for me to make the decision. I assure you it wasn't. I was only trying to do what was best for both of us. Anyway, you said you wanted to get out. Any idea where you want to go?'

Not missing the fact that there was a telling break in

her voice—as if she was striving to put on a brave face and show she didn't care that he'd refused to tell her about his mother's desertion—Hal lifted his shoulders in a shrug even as his heart ached to tell her *everything*.

'I don't care. Anywhere that's not here would be a good start. If I was mobile I'd go for a run, or even a walk. I can't do that so I'll leave it up to you to come up with an idea of what to do. I just hate being cooped up like this.'

Flipping one of her burnished copper plaits over her shoulder, Kit surprised him with a smile. The sight was like a welcome glimpse of the sun coming out on a day that was cloudy and grey, and it didn't fail to warm Hal's heart.

'Well, there's no need to stay here feeling like you're a prisoner in your own home,' she announced. 'We should get out and get some fresh air. Leave it to me. I'll mull over where we can go while I get you your breakfast.'

Kit's resolution to distance herself emotionally and physically from Hal was severely tested that morning. She'd been able to tell the instant he'd come into the kitchen that he hadn't had much sleep. And it wasn't just because he hadn't had a shave. His lean, carved features looked almost haggard, and she couldn't help feeling guilty that her decision not to spend the rest of the night with him was the cause. *She hadn't had a lot of sleep herself for the same reason.*

And when he'd struggled to put his sweater back on, after inadvertently donning it back to front, the sight of his broad tanned shoulders and heavenly chest had made her insides flip at the memory of how incredible it had felt to make love with him. Without a doubt she knew that the act of passion they'd shared had been not just irresistible but *necessary* too.

Not that Kit had needed reminding. Her body still ached and tingled from Hal's ardent attentions and she longed to be able to share with him how he'd made her feel. She'd never felt particularly attractive or sensual, but he had helped her feel both of those things last night. Now she was torn between following her heart and her finely honed instinct for self-preservation, and therein lay the dilemma.

Not wanting to dwell on her own inner turmoil above seeing to Hal's desire to get out of the apartment for a while, she had an idea. As he finished his breakfast at the table she said brightly, 'I've thought of where we can go.'

'Have you?'

Throwing down his napkin with a weary air, he didn't sound remotely interested or impressed, and she could tell that a bit of downheartedness and despair had crept in. It made her all the more determined to lift his spirits and proceed with the plan she'd come up with.

'Yes, I have. I just want to clear away the breakfast things and then we can go. I think we're going to need our jackets and scarves because it looks quite cold and blustery out there this morning.' She glanced out of the window at the overcast skies and at the windblown leaves that were occasionally flying past, plastering themselves to the panes of glass. 'Would you like to read the newspaper while I stack the dishwasher? I found it on the mat this morning.'

'I may as well.'

Clearly resigned, Hal didn't let his returning glance

linger for too long, Kit noticed—as if he'd resolved not to be quite so friendly. The mere thought cut her to the quick. The sooner they were out in the open the better. It would give them both a chance to clear their heads and it would be good to blow the cobwebs away—especially as neither of them had had much sleep last night.

The household tasks completed, Kit moved across the kitchen to where Hal still sat perusing the newspaper. Without asking his permission, she plucked it out of his hands.

'Hey! What do you think you're doing?' His expression was furious.

'You said you wanted to go out, remember? You can read the newspaper when we get back.'

Deftly folding the broadsheet, she dropped it down onto the table. Then, taking a firm hold of the wheelchair's handles, she turned it forthrightly towards the door.

Still seething, Hal remarked sardonically, 'I was in the middle of reading an interesting article about the number of people losing their jobs…particularly *women*. Apparently it's a real problem.'

'Is it really? I don't expect it will be a problem for very long. Not with women's ingenuity and resourcefulness at finding replacement situations. We're very good at rising to a challenge and getting ourselves out of a tough spot…it comes from centuries of having to take care of not so ingenious and resourceful men!'

'You should be a comedian. Anyone ever tell you that?'

Helplessly, Kit's lips twitched in amusement. 'No. They haven't. But I'll bear it in mind should I ever find myself without a job. I can turn my hand to most things if I have to.'

'Hmm...'

His shoulders had stiffened. It definitely irked him whenever she got the better of him, she noticed.

'Presumably we're travelling to our destination by car?' he asked, swiftly changing the subject.

'No, we're not. I'm going to push you in your chair.'

'I don't think so.' He twisted round with a belligerent glare that might have intimidated her if she hadn't known better. 'If we're not going in the car then I'll take my crutches and walk,' he declared.

'Not today you won't, sunshine.'

They were travelling down the spacious hallway with its gleaming parquet flooring, and when she reached the coatstand at the end Kit reached up for Hal's chocolate-coloured suede jacket and briskly handed it to him.

'I want you to get out into the fresh air, but we're going too far for you to use crutches. By the way, have you got a scarf? I don't want you getting cold.'

'I'm warning you, Katherine with a K, if you persist in treating me like some dull-witted imbecile then I'll call a cab to take me wherever I want to go and I won't let you know when I'll be back. Then you'll be forced to stay here on your own and soberly contemplate at what point you pushed me too far!'

Kit had never seen a man look so adorable when he was angry, but Hal Treverne cornered the market in sheer adorability in her opinion—*whatever* his mood. However, right then she didn't think he would appreciate her telling him so. The reason he was angry, she guessed, was because he couldn't get around with the effortless ease he was accustomed to and it made him feel vulnerable.

She knew how frightening that was for anyone who strove to be in sole command of his destiny—especially when events didn't always pan out as he wanted them to. Kit found it easy to empathise because she'd often felt that same sense of frightening vulnerability too. Especially when she'd lived at home with her mother and daily anticipated the rollercoaster existence they were living spinning even further out of control...

'I don't want to make you mad at me,' she said.

Before she thought about the wisdom of her action she brought her hand down on the top of his head and lightly ruffled his hair. Just as she was about to draw away, Hal caught her by the wrist. Almost immediately his hold tightened.

'Then don't imagine that you're the one in charge— because you're *not*.'

Even as he warned her Kit saw that his golden eyes were no longer glinting with fury but with something else far more disturbing. Meeting his gaze, she felt as if she'd been steeped in a vat of warm honey.

'One kiss,' he murmured, the timbre of his voice lowering huskily. 'One kiss and I'll let you take me wherever you want to—even in this dratted wheelchair.'

She made a half-hearted attempt at freeing her wrist, but her arm had slackened weakly the moment Hal had taken it prisoner.

'I told you—I can't do that any more.' Even to her own ears her answer sounded less than convincing.

His dark brows beetled in a mocking frown. 'In my dictionary there's no such word as "can't", sweetheart.'

'I think you'll find that there is. Maybe not in yours,

but in most dictionaries the term is described as a contraction. Perhaps you need to update your volume?'

Even as she came back with the witty rejoinder Kit's heart was hammering, because she knew that this was one situation where she wouldn't get the better of him. Not this time.

'You're too clever for your own good, Kit Blessington. Now, shut up and let me kiss you.'

Pulling her down to him, he crushed her lips beneath the slightly rough, melting warmth of his own. With a surrendering gasp she allowed her mouth to be thoroughly captured, offering not the slightest resistance as his tongue swept its satin interior and his hands cupped her face. The taste and feel of him was like being given the keys to Nirvana. The pleasure he gave her was almost indescribable.

How was she supposed to keep to her resolve not to be intimate with him again? Hal Treverne was in her blood, like a raging fever that wouldn't be cooled, and Kit knew she was fast becoming addicted to him. More than that, she realised, she was deeply in love with him. The thought wrenched a partly shocked, partly despairing groan from her. Despite her heartfelt vow not to, it seemed she was intent on repeating her mother's reckless folly all over again.

'We should—we should get going,' she murmured.

With her legs decidedly unsteady, she stepped abruptly away from Hal and reached up to the hook on the coatstand for her warm sheepskin-lined jacket. Draping a purple scarf around her neck and loosely knotting it, she saw that Hal was fastening his suede jacket with a somewhat bemused expression on his face.

'That kiss was like having a warming dram of

whisky before we set out on our expedition into the cold.' He grinned. 'I can't pretend I won't be tempted to have another one on our return. Lead the way, Captain.'

With a charming, mocking salute, he defied her not to give him an argument.

CHAPTER TEN

THE WIND WAS particularly raw and unforgiving that day. As Kit briskly pushed Hal's wheelchair along the smooth concreted paths in the park she knew that being forced to be static wasn't helping him maintain his body's warmth. He would have hated it, but she wished she'd brought a rug to tuck round him. She'd be willing to endure his angry glares if it made him feel more comfortable.

As if reading her mind, Hal piped up, 'It's warmer than this climbing a glacier! I can't say I'm exactly bowled over by this expedition, Kit.'

'It's not an expedition. It's meant to be a pleasurable stroll. I know it's cold, but at least we're out in the fresh air. There's a charming little café at the other side of the park and we'll head over there soon. But first I think we should take a little exercise, don't you?'

His broad shoulders tensed as he turned round to observe her. His chiselled profile was far from amused.

'That's not very funny and I don't appreciate the joke.'

'I'm not mocking you, Hal.' Swallowing hard, Kit frowned in apology. 'I just want you to know that even though you can't get around like you normally do right now you can still have fun.'

'This is your idea of *fun*?'

'Anything can be fun if you have the right attitude. How about this, for instance? Make sure you're holding on.'

Taking a deep breath, she firmed her gloved hands round the wheelchair's handles and started to run at full pelt down the path. Fortunately the park was sparsely populated that morning, the path was wide, and the only person they passed was an elderly man walking his terrier. As the trees, lake and the benches on the path flew by she couldn't help laughing out loud. Inside, she was suddenly filled with the kind of joy she very rarely *if ever* felt. The discovery that it was immensely liberating going against the conformity of what people expected made her want to do it more often.

At first it seemed as though her madcap idea had stunned Hal into silence, but as she continued to push him at speed down the path, he shouted up to her, 'You are one crazy woman, Kit Blessington. Do you know that?'

'Are you having fun now?' she shouted back.

'Hell, yes! Can't you go any faster?'

Kit kept her promise and after making their way across to the other side of the park, out of breath and with her cheeks healthily pink, she took Hal to the café she'd mentioned for coffee and cake. The table they selected had a wonderful view of the sparkling lake—at last the sun had started to shine, making the blue-green water shimmer like diamonds. Gratefully curling her hands round her hot mug of coffee, and observing the heightened colour in the sculpted planes of Hal's handsome face as well, she knew a delicious sense of well-being that she wished she could bottle.

'Feeling a bit warmer now?' She smiled.

'I feel strangely like I've run a marathon.' The corner of his lips quirked beguilingly. 'Well...maybe a *half* marathon. You were right—that *was* fun.'

'Good. I had fun too. What's the fruitcake like?'

Hal was already shaking his head and returning the slice of cake he'd just taken a bite out of to his plate. 'Nowhere near the standard of yours. Six out of ten, I'd say.'

'And mine is...?'

'You're a bad girl, fishing for compliments like that.'

His voice lowered to a smoky cadence that heated Kit's blood and made the tips of her breasts prickle hotly inside her bra.

'But I'll still tell you. You're definitely a ten. I can't fault you, it seems.'

'We're talking about my cake...*aren't we?*'

'Are we?' Leaning across the table, Hal reached for her hand, lifted it to his lips and kissed it. 'The truth is you make me giddy. The line between reality and fantasy always seems to be blurred when I look at you, Kit.'

He meant every word. Her presence in his life was growing more and more essential to his well-being—and not just because she had appeared in his life exactly when he needed her. As he gazed into her bewitching summer-blue eyes his heart gently pounded inside his chest. He'd climbed mountains and navigated raging rivers in his search for thrills and excitement. He had taken recording artists to the pinnacle of their careers because he'd believed in them when no one else had, where no one would take the risk of backing an unknown. But nothing he'd done or achieved in his life could beat what he felt when he was next to this woman…no wonder she made him giddy!

Kit's face flushed even pinker at his comment.

'It's probably the fresh air and the unexpected speed at which I pushed you in the chair that's made you giddy,' she quipped, as if determined not to believe his declaration had been generated by any other reason than that.

There was one other younger couple in the café with them, and when Hal reached for Kit's hand and kissed it he noticed over her shoulder that the girl was sending him a pleased smile of acknowledgement—as if he'd suddenly been granted entry into an elite and prestigious club. *It was a good feeling.* Suddenly he didn't mind if people looked at him and Kit and imagined they were a bona-fide couple. In fact he hoped that they *did*. His sister Sam would be over the moon that he was even open to the idea.

'Will you tell me more about the married man you had a liaison with?' he asked, suddenly needing to know.

'All right…'

Even though the question had clearly discomfited her, Hal was pleased that Kit wasn't going to shy away from answering it.

'I told you it was my twenty-first birthday and my friends had taken me to a club? Well, there was a restaurant upstairs, where we had a meal, and he was one of the waiters there. Anyway, he was very attentive to all of us, but for some reason he was extra-attentive to me. Towards the end of the evening, when he'd finished his shift, he came to find me. I'm afraid I'd had a little too much to drink in a bid to cheer myself up, because turning twenty-one and not having anyone who mattered in my life except my mum had made me feel rather low, and when he offered to take me home I let him.'

She glanced away for a moment, as if cautious about revealing too much and perhaps being judged for it.

'Anyway, he helped me into the house, where I had a room upstairs. He—he started kissing me. I should have made him stop, but I was drunk and hardly knew what I was doing. I stupidly told him that I needed to lie down and he led me over to the bed.' Ruefully shaking her head, Kit grimaced. 'To cut a long story short, he had sex with me, and afterwards…just before he left… he told me he was married. He took great pleasure in telling me, I remember. That's it…end of story. In truth, I had a lucky escape.'

'And you didn't report him to the police?'

'Why? He just took what he thought was on offer. The whole fiasco was *my* fault. I did everything I shouldn't have. I'd had too much to drink and I let a stranger take me home. The only sensible thing I managed to do that night was to insist he wore protection. Luckily he'd brought some with him. It obviously wasn't the first time he'd taken advantage of a woman who really ought to have known better.'

Kit's blue-eyed glance was unwaveringly direct.

'You're probably wondering why I acted so stupidly. The truth is I let my guard down that night because I was flattered by his attention. Sometimes we all want to be liked and admired, don't we? That's all that sorry episode was about—a very human need to be noticed by someone.'

'But you let him take your virginity, Kit. That's the

saddest part of the story. I wish you could have given it to someone who saw it as the most precious gift a woman can give to a man.' *It grieved Hal more than he could possibly say that she hadn't.*

'So do I.' She fell silent for a moment. 'Anyway, now I've shared my story, will you tell me about your mother, Hal?'

As painful as the topic was, if he wanted things to progress further with Kit then Hal knew he couldn't avoid speaking about it any longer. Suddenly it was imperative that she grew to trust him—especially after what she'd just told him—and in order for her to do that he had to have the courage to open up to her about his past. *Who knew?* If he took the risk it might open the door to the possibility of them enjoying a genuine relationship. Hal at least had to try.

Holding her gaze across the table, he gave her a tentative smile. Did he really have the courage to be vulnerable enough to confess the wreckage of his past to this woman?

'All right, then. I'll tell you about her,' he agreed.

Her eyes widening, Kit gently loosened her hand from his and sat back in her seat to give him her full attention.

'My mother was very beautiful,' he went on, his hand tunnelling restlessly through his hair for a moment. 'And her bewitching looks drew men to her like bees to honey. My dad is a wealthy landowner, and even though he was mad about her when they first met and asked her to marry him his property and his estate always came first. She didn't appear to mind that too much. She loved the fact that he was landed gentry as well as being rich, but she didn't understand why he chose to work at all when he didn't have to. If she'd troubled to find out, she would have soon learned that taking care of the estate and the people who worked for him to maintain it was a matter of fierce pride to him. The estate has been in the family since the sixteenth century, and my dad wasn't going to be the one that saw it fall to rack and ruin, as he'd say. The charities he supported were also hugely important to him, and he'd hoped that my mother would see how being associated with them might help her. Given her PR background, he thought she might be able to help fundraise and organise events and might even enjoy it.

'He encouraged her to try and forge a good relationship with the staff on the estate and get to know them a little. To sum it up, my father believed that she needed a purpose…at least until children came along. She'd been flitting in and out of PR work when they'd first met, but her heart wasn't really in it. Turned out that she had her own ideas about what the "lady of the house" should do, and when she moved onto the estate with my dad it became clear that it wasn't very much.

'She couldn't hack the isolation of the countryside. She was a city girl through and through and she hated being alone when my dad was taking care of his business on the estate—especially as she craved attention round the clock. In a very rare and honest moment my father once told me that he'd hoped when she had me and Sam she would settle down a bit, be more content with her lot. But instead of becoming devoted to her family she grew more and more restless and started to have affairs.'

Grimacing, Hal shook his head.

'At first my father turned a blind eye, hoping she

would grow tired of her soulless behaviour and realise what she had at home...two children who adored her, and a husband who loved her enough to forgive her destructive behaviour and also hoped that given time she would change for the better.'

Clearing his throat, Hal picked up his mug of coffee and took a swig. At the same time he found himself examining Kit's pensive expression to try and gauge what she must be thinking about his faithless mother and his perhaps *too* patient, some might say foolishly deluded father. Henry Treverne Senior was a man who had never given up hope that his wife would come to see the error of her ways and be content just to be his partner and mother to their children.

'Unfortunately she never *did*...change for the better, I mean.' He shrugged. 'When Sam and I were nine and seven respectively she ran off with an Italian count and relocated to Venice. She never kept in touch, even though my father regularly wrote to her and told her how much Sam and I were missing her.' Hal bit down on his lip as a familiar scissor of pain jack-knifed through his heart at the memory.

Again he cleared his throat and took another swig of coffee. 'About six years ago—just about the time I started to make a name for myself in the music industry—my father was notified by the Italian authorities that she'd been killed in a car accident. Apparently the Count's twenty-one-year-old son from a previous marriage had been driving the car at the time and also lost his life. It was common knowledge in Venice that he and my mother had been having an affair. Doesn't make for a very pretty story, does it?'

'That's so sad. For *all* of you.' Her face paling a little,

Kit breathed out a soft, heartfelt sigh. 'Do you mind if I ask who looked after you and your sister when she left?'

Hal grimaced. 'A series of not very reliable nannies, I'm afraid. One or two of them might have stayed, given the chance, but my father didn't think any of them were good enough to mind his children. He was always finding fault with them for some reason or other. The truth is—courtesy of my beautiful, faithless mother, I think—he started to believe that women on the whole were fickle and not to be depended on. As soon as Sam and myself were old enough, he packed us off to boarding school.'

Taking another sip of coffee, he realised it was now practically cold. 'Ugh.' Wiping the back of his hand across his mouth, he returned the mug to the table, his avid gaze alighting on Kit. 'We could be close…me and my father, I mean. But he couldn't see why I wanted to leave and branch out on my own in a career when I was going to one day inherit the estate and title from him. He still doesn't understand my reasons for wanting to be completely independent and neither does he see—in *his* words—why I "recklessly" risk my life in pursuing extreme sports.'

Kit's smooth brow puckered in a frown. 'Is that why he didn't come and visit you in the hospital after your accident? You said that he'd e-mailed you saying "pride comes before a fall".'

With any other woman he would have been surprised she should remember such a detail, but *not* with Kit. Hal heaved a sigh. To be honest, he wanted to shake off that painful illustration of the chasm that had grown between him and his father but he just couldn't.

'Trouble is he was right, you know? The only reason I agreed to that stupid bet with Rigden was because I *had* to prove I was better than him. Sometimes I *am* proud…too proud to see reason and let common sense rule.'

Ruefully he tapped his knuckles against his cast. 'This injury being a case in point. But my dad's proud as well—too proud to admit that sometimes he might be wrong. He *should* have come to see me in the hospital!'

With a tender smile, Kit nodded her agreement. 'Yes, he should have. But perhaps he was unsure how his visit would be received by you—whether it would be welcome or not if there had been previous disagreement and tension between you? When you spend too much time apart from someone it's very easy to believe that you know them so well you can predict how they're going to react when you see them again. You don't consider that they might have moved on from their old behaviour or changed for the better. When was the last time you actually spent any time with your dad, Hal?'

He sensed the heat rise in his face even before he started to speak. Kit's words had definitely given him pause. 'I don't know…a few months, I suppose. I know that sounds bad, but I've always been too busy to organise anything. Besides…' he shrugged a shoulder '…I got fed up with listening to his criticisms every time we happened to speak.'

Leaning towards him, Kit gently laid her hand over his. Her blue eyes were so captivating that Hal temporarily forgot that he was aggrieved with his dad. It was like gazing back into the most serene and calm lake.

'Would you like to go and see him? If he won't come to you, maybe you should go to him?'

Ever since he'd had his accident in Aspen it had been

eating away at him that his father hadn't shown any evidence that he cared. Resentment was a bitter companion, and it was only apt to grow worse if not dealt with, he knew. Kit's suggestion that he make a conciliatory move and go and visit his father was so obvious, so eminently sensible, that he knew he couldn't resist it. Reliving some of the tensions of his past with her just now had made him suddenly yearn to make amends. Losing one parent was bad enough—never mind allowing your relationship with the remaining one to deteriorate so much that you barely spoke to each other.

'Once again your astute insight has floored me, Kit,' he told her. 'You're right…I should go and see my dad. It's crazy that I've put it off for so long. Will you drive me?'

Immediately she withdrew her hand from his and frowned. 'Of course I will, but…where does he live?'

'Hertfordshire.'

'And when would you like to make the trip?'

'I want to go today. We should strike while the iron's hot—before I have the chance to think about it too much and talk myself out of it.'

'Shouldn't you ring your dad first and check that he'll be home?'

An irresistibly boyish grin split his lips wide. 'I probably should, but I won't. I'd rather just turn up and surprise him. Even if he's out, his housekeeper will let us in. He'll come back sooner or later. By the way—we ought to pack an overnight bag. It's too late to travel there and back today.'

Slowly, Kit nodded. 'Well, if you think that's all right, then of course we can go today. But first of all

I'd like to ice that knee for you, and then you should rest for a while. We can go after that.'

'I can rest in the car. After all, I don't have to worry about driving.'

Zipping up his jacket, Hal was surprised at how enthused he suddenly felt about the idea of making amends with his father. It would also be good to see his childhood home again, despite his fractured upbringing. Falteringham House, the Treverne estate, was breathlessly stunning, and he'd honestly missed it. Any man would be proud to have connections with such beauty, grandeur and history. But most of all Hal realised he was looking forward to introducing it to Kit.

'Come on, Nurse Blessington,' he urged with a smile. 'Let's get going, shall we?'

Kit had honed a helpful ability to get packing down to a fine art. She'd *had* to when she was so often moving from place to place for work. But when she stepped out of her bedroom to find Hal patiently leaning against the wall on his crutches, a classy leather tote down by his feet, she couldn't help smiling.

'That was quick. I see you're all packed and ready. I was just about to come and find you to help.'

'No need. I'm nothing if not prepared,' he quipped, an irresistible twinkle in his chameleon hazel eyes. 'I often have to jet off somewhere at the drop of a hat, so it pays to at least have one well-equipped bag ready. I see you've changed your hairstyle… I have to say I approve. The schoolgirl plaits were definitely cute, but I much prefer it when you look like one of Millais's models.'

After swapping her jeans and shirt for a smart pair of black trousers and a dove-grey Arran sweater Kit had quickly dismantled her plaits and shaken her hair loose. Once again the fiery copper waves tumbled freely over her shoulders, and they helped give her a sense of confidence she found herself suddenly in dire need of. If her one claim to beauty couldn't help her to that end, then what *could*?

The prospect of meeting Hal's upper-crust father, as well as visiting his ancestral family home, was seriously daunting. Although she was all but certain that it would—at last—dash any pointless hope she might be secretly nurturing that she could have a future with him. Best she just keep on reminding herself that if she continued to work hard then one day soon she would have the precious home of her own that she longed for. And she wouldn't have to depend on any man—even if she was head over heels in love with him—to provide it for her.

It was close to dusk by the time they reached the end of a long tree-lined drive and pulled up outside the esteemed manor house where Hal had grown up. Surrounded by lush parkland, the building was frighteningly imposing, Kit saw, even in the gloomy half-light of the day. Its Elizabethan windows and stone turrets made it look almost ethereal. And, apart from the late-afternoon birdsong, the silence that cloaked the area was eerily tangible. When she switched off the car's ignition and turned round to observe her passenger in the seat that she'd extended for him, so he could stretch out his injured leg, she saw immediately that his handsome face looked perturbed.

'What's up?' she asked. 'I'm sorry if it was a little

bumpy coming down the drive. You're not in pain, I hope?'

'Unless you have the power to go back to Elizabethan times and predict that we'll be driving round in engine-driven motor cars in five hundred years' time, so we had better level the road, there's not much you can do about the bumpy drive, I'm afraid. The surface has always been uneven and slightly bowed. And, in answer to your second question, I'm not in pain. But thanks for asking.'

Clamping down on her automatic response—*It's my job to ask how you're feeling*—Kit somehow shaped her lips into a smile. 'Anyway, it looks like an amazing house. It must have been wonderful, growing up with so much space around you. The places me and my mum lived in were always so cramped and small.'

Hal's gaze narrowed interestedly. 'I've been meaning to ask you…where does your mother live now? Is she on her own or does she have a partner?'

It had never been easy to talk about her mum at the best of times, and it wasn't any easier now. Inevitably, even though she had forged a life of her own and didn't regret it, Kit couldn't help sometimes feeling guilty that she didn't make herself as available to her as she'd used to. But the last time they'd spoken on the phone, Elizabeth Blessington had told her that she'd tentatively been dating the widower who lived next door to the building where her little flat was housed. It was early days yet, she'd stated, her tone sounding uncharacteristically cautious, but she had high hopes that it might blossom into something special.

Tucking some hair behind her ear, Kit stopped frowning and lifted her gaze back to Hal's.

'She lives in London and, yes, she lives alone. But she's recently started dating a widower who lives nearby, so I'm sure she has company from time to time. Anyway, shouldn't we go and find out if your dad is in? I can wheel you in your chair, or would you prefer to use your walking aids?'

'I'll use the crutches. I'd prefer to confront my dad when I'm standing upright.' His lips thinned ruefully.

'"Confront"?'

'Wrong word. Come on, let's go in.'

As they stood outside the imposing gabled front door Kit stole a glance at Hal to try and ascertain how he was feeling. His carved handsome face never failed to make her heart race, and it raced even more now because she'd intuited that he had mixed feelings about coming home to see his father again. She prayed the meeting would go well. The last thing he needed was to feel it hadn't been a success.

'If I didn't have to hold onto these damned crutches I'd hold your hand,' he said gruffly, a riveting dimple appearing at the side of his mouth.

Her insides cartwheeled pleasurably. 'I'm here for you, Hal. You don't have to worry.' Gently, Kit touched her hand to the back of his chocolate-brown jacket.

At that very same moment the door opened. A distinguished-looking man who looked to be in his sixties appeared. He had liberally greying dark hair that must once have been as strong and lustrous as the hair of the man standing beside her, and was dressed in casual country tweeds with a waxed jacket. Possessed of the same compelling hazel-eyed gaze as the younger man, he stared at Hal as though being confronted by a ghost.

Kit dropped her hand.

'Hello, Dad. Thought I'd surprise you.' His son greeted him diffidently.

'Why in God's name didn't you ring to let me know you were coming?' the other man responded.

He had the kind of resonant, booming voice usually attributed to distinguished actors who performed Shakespeare, and Kit didn't mind admitting that it startled her.

'I'll turn round and go back to London if it's inconvenient,' Hal countered immediately, unable to keep the hurt from his tone.

'Of course it's not inconvenient. If it's a surprise you hoped for then you've succeeded. I didn't mean that it was an unwelcome one. Come in, come in. It's clear you can't stand there for long on those crutches. It can hardly be good for you.'

'I'll help you,' Kit said quickly, her hand once again going to Hal's broad back to reassure him.

'And who might *you* be, young lady?' the older man asked pointedly, making no bones about looking her up and down.

Casting aside the uncomfortably warm sensation of self-consciousness that spread throughout her body, she determinedly lifted her head and silently defied him to find fault or look down his aristocratic nose at her for even a second.

'My name is Kit Blessington. Your son hired me to give him some practical help while he recuperates from his accident.'

'*Did* he, indeed?' There was a definite suggestion of a mocking smile around the mouth whose upper lip was decorated by a dark military-style moustache. 'Well, I'm Sir Henry Treverne—Hal's father—as I'm sure you've gleaned by now. It's good to know that my son had the foresight to get himself some help and support when he needed it, for once. He usually insists on doing most things alone, but I'm glad that on this occasion common sense prevailed.'

'Thanks for the vote of confidence,' Hal interjected drolly. The strain of maintaining his upright pose with the walking aids was suddenly reflected on his furrowed brow. 'I hate to break up the party, but can we go in now? And my companion and I wouldn't say no to a cup of coffee and a sandwich. It's been a long, tiring drive.'

'If you and Ms Blessington make your way into the family drawing room, I'll go and find my housekeeper and get her to organise it. Now, come in from the cold and go and sit in front of the fire to warm up.'

Before he turned to follow his father inside the house Hal deliberately caught Kit's eye and gave her a reassuring wink, as if he already knew that this visit wasn't going to be an easy one for her either…

CHAPTER ELEVEN

A WARM FIRE was indeed blazing invitingly in the marble fireplace as they entered the family drawing room. It was a strange feeling, coming back to the room Hal had sat in so many times over the years with his father and sister…almost a surreal sensation—as if the past was nothing but a dream he'd conjured up. It was literally years since the three of them had spent any proper time together, and it was growing more and more unlikely that they ever *would*. The loving, caring family unit that he'd longed for them to become after his mother had left had never really become a reality.

Not liking the sombre direction his thoughts were taking him in—especially when he'd resolved to heal the rift with his father—Hal made his way across the expansive stone floor, liberally covered with hand-crafted Persian rugs, and carefully lowered himself onto one of the leather couches. Kit stayed close by him to help. As he sat she took his crutches away and laid them down on the floor, where he could easily reach them. Then, with a self-conscious smile she moved away.

It wasn't the reaction he'd anticipated. Whether she acknowledged it or not, there was a definite bond between them now, and in his mind their lovemaking last night had sealed that bond. He was no longer just a client she was working for, and she was no longer simply his hired help. With every fibre of Hal's being he ached for more intimate contact—or at least for them to be easy enough with each other that they would automatically sit together. With that in mind, he gestured for her to come back and join him. It was akin to receiving a blow when he saw that her pretty blue eyes were reticent.

'I'd better not. Your father might think it's not very professional of me to sit next to you. He might think that I—that we—' She was unable to finish the sentence and her cheeks coloured helplessly. As if desperately needing a distraction, she glanced round for a suitable place to sit. Selecting one of the armchairs positioned opposite Hal, she finally made herself comfortable.

'That we are up to no good?' he finished for her, his lips twisting wryly. 'I *hate* that expression. Even if he doesn't approve, do you think that's going to stop me from wanting you or showing *him* that I want you?'

Exasperation was close to getting the better of Hal, because the need to hold Kit close had been mercilessly taunting him all day. In contrast, she had been unbelievably composed and pragmatic. How on earth was he going to convince her that he was in earnest about how he felt? That he didn't just want a meaningless fling but something far more serious?

The depth and breadth of his intentions took him aback. Shaken, he shrugged off his jacket and dropped it onto the cushion beside him.

'I told you that I can't do this…that I—' She stopped.

'Need to be sensible?'

'I know that you don't want to hear that, but—'

'My housekeeper, Mary, is going to bring us in some refreshments, and after that she's going to go and get your rooms ready. I presume you and Miss Blessington *are* staying the night, Hal?'

His father's timing couldn't have been *worse,* Hal thought irritably. Yes, he wanted them to build bridges with him—that was why he was here—but equally he wanted to put things right between him and Kit—to get her to see that he wasn't the spoilt playboy used to getting his own way that she might secretly fear he was… not a man who wouldn't hesitate to use her and then cast her aside just as her mother's ex-boyfriends had done to *her.* But it looked as if that particular conversation would have to wait until later, when they could be alone.

'Yes, we are. I'd rather not ask Kit to drive us back to town tonight. And, by the way, I'm going to need a downstairs room—and so is Kit, in case I need her.'

'That won't be a problem. That's settled, then. So, how have things been since the accident?' his father asked, taking a seat in the high-backed armchair next to Kit.

The question was posed in the familiar non-committal and unemotional tone that Hal knew only too well. It was clearly too much to expect him to ask how he was *feeling*. Probably the only reason he'd referred to his son's injury was so that he could once again tell him how reckless he'd been, proving his opinion that pride came before a fall to be unerringly right.

Unable to help himself, Hal immediately made it his mission to disappoint him. 'Things are good—much better than I expected, given the debilitating nature of my injury.' Glancing over at Kit, he was surprised to see that her hands were folded almost demurely in her lap and her eyes were downcast, as if she didn't want to draw particular attention to herself…as if she believed she should be as unobtrusive as possible. Was it because coming face to face with the imposing grandeur of his home and meeting his father had overwhelmed her? Perhaps it had even made her nurse a feeling of inferiority? The mere thought that she might be entertaining such a self-deprecating idea made him see red. Apart from his sister, Hal didn't know one other woman who could match her for sheer class…

'In fact I went for a run in the park this morning. Didn't I, Kit?'

'This is a serious matter. I don't think it's something you should be joking about, Henry.'

The disapproving glance crossing his father's features, plus the more formal use of his name, made Hal bristle. 'Isn't it? If we can't laugh at the vicissitudes of life sometimes then we'll all be permanently addicted to tranquillisers merely to help us survive. Personally, I'd rather feel the pain than dull it or pretend it isn't there.'

'Your son wasn't entirely joking, Sir Henry,' Kit interjected calmly, leaping to Hal's defence. 'We *did* go for a run in the park. At least, *I* ran as I pushed him in his wheelchair.'

'Did you, indeed?' Staring at her, his father blustered, 'Did you *really* think that was a good idea when my son already has a broken leg, young woman? What if he had fallen out of the chair and hurt himself even more?'

'There was no chance of that. For goodness' sake, I'm an adult, not a child, and Kit was only trying to cheer me up.' Hal was rigid with anger. 'In any case, why is the thought of having some fun so alien to you,

Father? Not everything in life has to be so damn serious. Do you even *know* the concept of relaxation?'

To his surprise, the other man looked almost crestfallen.

'The truth is I probably don't,' he answered quietly. 'I've always felt that my responsibility for raising a family and leaving a healthy legacy for my children after I'm gone was paramount...just as my forebears did. *Too* serious a matter to take lightly and relax.'

'You drive yourself too hard. Sam and I have been independent for a long time now, Dad. I'd rather you stopped working so hard and just thought about what you wanted for yourself. Take some time out. Go on an extended holiday. You've got plenty of people working for you who could take care of things in your absence. Falteringham isn't going to go to rack and ruin if you're not here, as you fear it might. You should make a new priority to have some fun. Maybe even find yourself a nice woman?'

As Henry Treverne Senior's downturned mouth nudged into a surprising smile the drawing room door opened. Transporting a tray laden with cups, saucers, a plate of sandwiches and a full cafetière, the housekeeper—Mary—came into the room. She was a statuesque middle-aged woman with broad hips, bobbed brown hair and a clear open face that in her youth might have been called pretty.

Aware that they hadn't been introduced—his father's last housekeeper had retired a few months ago—Hal automatically gave the woman a welcoming smile. 'You must be Mary?' he said as she laid the tray down on the walnut coffee table in front of him. 'I'm Henry.' He held out his hand to shake hers.

Clearly surprised at a welcome she hadn't expected, the woman slid her palm into his and smiled back.

'It's nice to meet you, Mr Treverne. Your father is always singing your praises. I'm so sorry about your accident, by the way. But I'm sure it won't be too long before you're back on your feet again. Anyway, help yourself to coffee and sandwiches. If you want any more do let me know. In the meantime I'll be getting your rooms ready.'

When she'd departed, his father sat back in his chair and sighed.

'She's a breath of fresh air, that woman. I honestly don't know what I'd do without her.'

This frank confession, coming straight after Mary had told him that his father was always singing his praises, doubly stunned Hal. It opened the door to a distinct possibility that he had unfairly misjudged the man. Shaking his head in wonder, he said, 'If you feel like that then all I can say is welcome back to the land of the living. Good for you, Dad.' Glancing across the room at Kit, he felt his heart warm when he saw that her pretty mouth was curving in what looked to be an approving smile. 'Why don't you come over here and tuck into some of these sandwiches?' he invited her. 'They look seriously good.'

'My son is right, Miss Blessington. Or perhaps you wouldn't mind if I called you Kit? You must be hungry after making that long drive from London. You should definitely eat something.'

'Thank you. I will.'

When she'd reached the table Hal couldn't resist reaching for her hand and squeezing it. She didn't immediately pull away, as he'd thought she might, even though her smile was somewhat tentative and shy. Catching the unspoken question in his father's eyes, he realised he was watching them. But Hal honestly didn't care that he'd witnessed the fact that the relationship between him and Kit wasn't *entirely* a professional one. There was suddenly a great desire in him to be transparent for once—to be honest and open about his feelings and take the consequences, no matter how difficult or challenging they might be...

A short while later Kit was returning from the bathroom, just about to open the drawing room door to enter, when she heard Sir Henry's deeply resonant voice saying to his son, 'I must say your suggestion that I take an extended break sounds like a good one, Hal. I know I can rely on the staff here to take care of things in my absence. And while we're on the subject, have you had any more thoughts about one day coming home to take over the estate? I know you probably don't want to hear it, but I'm not getting any younger, and Falteringham needs some young blood in it again. Perhaps you need to think about marrying and having a family? Are you seeing any nice girls who might be suitable at the moment? The estate is your heritage, as well as your home, and I'd like you to help take it forward into the twenty-first century with a family of your own beside you.'

Outside the door, Kit froze and held her breath.

'Given that I've had a lot of time on my hands lately to reflect on things,' she heard Hal reply, 'you and the estate haven't been far from my mind. Yes, I would like to come back one day and take over the reins, with a wife and children of my own by my side...but just not right now. I'll know when the time is right.'

'Any idea when that might be?'

There was a pause, and then Hal sighed. 'No, Dad. I'm afraid you're just going to have to be patient.'

With her heart clamouring distressingly, Kit took a deep breath in and shakily curved her hand round the doorknob....

Dropping her holdall onto the end of the elegantly dressed half-tester bed in the room Mary had shown her into, Kit drew her hands down over her face and sighed heavily. She felt emotionally wrung out and weary to the bone. Even though she'd got through the rest of the evening without regretting that she'd agreed to Hal's request to take him back to his ancestral home, because it looked as if his father and he were honestly resolved on healing the rift between them, she was in utter turmoil about the discussion she'd heard between Hal and his father about him returning home one day to Falteringham House and assuming the ancestral role he'd be inheriting with a wife and children by his side.

Her memory of the conversation was upsettingly fixated on Sir Henry's enquiry as to whether Hal was seeing any 'nice' or 'suitable' girls at the moment. Nothing could have made her feel more out of place. Not just out of place, but heartsick, because she was in love with a man who was so clearly out of her league that it was pure fantasy to imagine even for an instant that she might have a future with him. Unfortunately Kit *wasn't* one of those 'nice' and 'suitable' girls that Hal's father wanted for his son. And, that being so, she would probably nurse her hurt and regret at not being able to be with Hal for ever.

You're such a fool, Kit... How could you have been so stupid? You're your mother all over again!

Furiously berating herself, she buried her face in her hands and cried and cried until she felt she couldn't cry any more. There wasn't a single place in her body where she didn't ache for Hal. Everything about him—the way he looked and smiled, the warm, sensual scent of his body, even the way he teased and provoked her to distraction—had ensured Kit would be an addict for him for life. It was as though he'd put her under a spell that she'd never be free of, no matter how hard she might try.

But, since she couldn't have him, the only thing she could look forward to was the prospect of the little bolt-hole she'd been working towards for most of her life. Making it into a reality. Perhaps when she had that she might at least have the satisfaction of achieving the one thing that she'd set out to do to make her life better. As for having a meaningful relationship... It was something that wasn't even remotely likely. Not now. *Not when Hal Treverne had ruined any chance that she'd ever be whole enough for anyone else again.*

Slipping off her shoes, she wearily tugged her sweater over her head and threw it onto the bed. Then she turned and headed for the bathroom. Usually a long hot soak in the tub was her therapy of choice to help soothe her and put things into perspective when she'd had a bad day. But, knowing that wasn't going to be the case tonight, she opted for a shower instead. After that she intended to go straight to bed.

At Sir Henry's suggestion she would take the opportunity to have an early night because he and his son had 'a lot to talk about'. She wasn't to worry, he'd said, because he would help Hal to his bedroom and see that he got his medication if he needed it. There was no need for them to disturb her. Every word of that little speech had sliced through Kit's heart like a sharpened scythe, because it had only served to remind her that she was already becoming superfluous to Hal's needs. The fact was he had access to a raft of people he could call upon for help if he wanted to. His wealth pretty much saw to that. *Would he even miss her when the time came for her to leave?* Kit speculated forlornly.

Underneath the hot spray of the shower, she disproved the belief that she had no more tears left to cry and helplessly, despairingly, cried again.

When she finally emerged from the glass cubicle she felt shaken and drained to the core. She didn't even feel as if she had the energy to dry herself. Scared at how powerfully she seemed to be unravelling, she determinedly switched her focus to the practicalities of getting ready for bed. To that end, she brushed her teeth, properly dried her hair, then unpacked her holdall to retrieve the cosily warm pyjamas she'd brought with her. They were a lot more practical than the silk chemise she'd worn the night Hal had seduced her, but the sight of them did little to help alleviate her sorrow. They were just another reminder that she'd never know another night of passion with the man she loved again.

Turning out the elegant lamp next to the bed, wanting to shut out not just the day's events but everything that troubled her, she closed her eyes. All she could do now was pray for an unbroken night's sleep in which to recover her strength and to somehow find the will and the means to overcome her sorrow so she could carry on with life regardless. God knew her mother had had to do just that *more* than once. If she could do it, then so could her daughter...

In Kit's dream, someone was tapping on the door. The repetitive sound didn't seem to abate, and finally it pierced her already fitful sleep and made her realise it was no dream but solid, disturbing fact. Dazedly scrambling to sit up, she pushed back the silky curtain of hair that brushed her face and stared over at the door. All she could see beneath the edges was an unbroken sliver of dimmed light that came from the corridor outside. There was no evidence of anyone's feet moving. Her head felt fuzzy and she couldn't think straight. Icy fear had robbed her of the ability. Was she still dreaming? It was hard to tell.

When the tapping sound abruptly ceased, she sucked in a relieved breath and nervously glanced round the room. Perhaps it *had* been a dream after all?

The moonlight outside her window dappled the emerald-green counterpane that covered the bed with haunting shadows, and did the same to the various pieces of dark antique furniture that were arranged round the room. Kit's heart galloped in fear in case a ghost suddenly appeared. She was already frightened out of her wits enough, without having to contend with some ghostly apparition!

When another bout of tapping broke the uneasy silence that had descended, this time with a bit more force, Kit remembered that Hal's room was next door. What if he was in urgent need of her help? She was mortified that it hadn't registered before that the knocking on the door was probably coming from *him*.

Shoving aside the counterpane, she swung her legs

over the side of the bed and hurried across the rug-covered stone flags to open the door. Her heart was already bumping anxiously against her ribs even before she set eyes on the man who waited outside. When she did, her heart bumped even harder. He was sleepy-eyed and tousle-haired, with a fresh growth of dark beard studding his chiselled jaw, and gazing into Hal's golden eyes was like stumbling onto a never-to-be forgotten glimpse of heaven.

'What's wrong?' she asked.

His answer was a provocative lopsided grin. 'Nothing now that I'm looking at you, angel.'

The smoky cadence of his voice somehow transmitted itself to Kit's muscles and made them feel dangerously weak. 'How long have you been knocking on the door?' she asked huskily. 'I thought I was dreaming.'

'I wasn't keeping track of the time. I just thought I'd stay here until I wore you down with my dogged persistence, got you to come and see who it was and hopefully let me in.'

Unconsciously clutching her pyjama top, agitatedly twisting the material into a knot in the process, Kit stared at him in disbelief, suddenly realising the only reason he was standing was because he was using his crutches to help him. Hadn't his father had the sense to get his wheelchair for him? She'd left him the car keys and had strongly emphasised that he shouldn't let his son rely solely on his walking aids to get to his room. He'd already told her that the guest rooms on the ground floor were right at the back of the house.

'Are you crazy? You should *never* have stood out there for so long. You'll have to come in and sit down on the bed for a while.'

'That invitation is music to my ears, sweetheart. I'm certainly not going to argue.' He winced a little, as though the strain of standing upright had unquestionably taxed him.

Again Kit berated herself for not doing her job properly—for leaving him. It didn't matter that he'd been with his father...no one knew better than *she* did what he needed. The impassioned thought sent a scalding, searing heat surging through her bloodstream that was like a swell of molten honey.

Biting down on her lip, she waited until Hal had passed her before shutting the door behind them. She noted he was still dressed in the clothes he'd been wearing to travel in. She had no idea of the time but it was obvious he hadn't been to bed yet. What did he think he was doing, staying up so late, when his surgeon had told him it was extremely important he got as much rest as possible while his leg healed?

'That's better.' Expelling a grateful sigh, he dropped down onto the rumpled green counterpane and handed her his crutches. 'Can you put these somewhere?'

'Sure.' Kit laid them against the striped green couch at the end of the bed, where they would be easily accessible. Then, folding her arms over her chest, she asked, 'Why on earth have you stayed up so late? Is there something you want to discuss that can't wait until the morning?'

His avid gaze intensifying a little, for a long moment Hal looked to be deep in thought. 'As a matter of fact, there is. But first I wanted to tell you something. My dad and I have been having a father and son talk—probably the first genuine discussion we've had for years. God knows it's long overdue. Turns out he doesn't think

I'm such a disaster after all. In fact he tells me he's more than a little awed by my success *and* my courage at pursuing my "hair-raising stunts" as he calls them— even though he can't always understand it. He's always thought that the reason I'm so reckless is because I don't value my life enough—that I must be suffering from some sort of depression brought about by my mother leaving when I was little. That seriously grieves him.

'He blames himself for not being there for me as often as he would have liked after she left, and he said that he wished it could have been different. But as well as making sure he's protecting mine and Sam's legacy he's so focused on taking care of the estate and the people who work for him because it's their livelihood too. He has to make those things his priority. Who could have predicted that he'd be so honest with me? You were right when you said I should come to see him, Kit. I'm glad that I did. Hearing the truth about how he really feels about me has helped lay a lot of the ghosts from my past that have haunted me to rest. Like any good parent, he just wanted the best for his children—even if I couldn't always see that that was his intention. Anyway, it feels good to clear the air and have the chance to repair things.'

'Then I suppose I shouldn't moan at you for staying up so late, since something good has come out it. But I don't think you should stay up for much longer. Not unless you intend to spend the whole of tomorrow resting and taking it easy. I think it's time you turned in and went to bed.'

One corner of Hal's engaging mouth lifted intriguingly. 'That brings me nicely to the main reason I knocked on your door sweetheart. I do indeed need to go to bed—but not on my own. I'd much rather have some company tonight and the company I want and need most in the world—not just for tonight—is *you*, Kit.'

Nothing could have prepared Kit for the dizzying joy that swept through her at his unexpected confession. In fact her feelings so overwhelmed her that she couldn't find the words or the actions to express how much they meant to her. But tainting her unexpected happiness was the distressing memory of the conversation she'd overheard between Hal and his father about him taking up his inheritance.

'I *can't* be the company you need most in the world, Hal,' she said soberly. 'Not when one day soon you'll be married to someone else…someone much more suitable than I am.'

'What on earth are you talking about? Who told you I'm soon going to be married to someone else?'

'It's obvious, isn't it? I didn't realise the extent and importance of your family legacy until I came here. It's understandable that you'll need to marry someone from your own class when one day you're going to inherit this estate.'

Frowning, Hal stared at her as though she were speaking a foreign language he didn't understand. Then comprehension dawned on him.

'Did you by any chance overhear a conversation between me and my dad? Specifically the part where he asked me if I would one day come back to take up my inheritance?'

Feeling uncomfortably guilty, Kit nodded. 'I did. I didn't mean to eavesdrop. It's just that I was on my way back from the bathroom and your father—well, he doesn't speak quietly.'

To her astonishment, Hal threw back his head and laughed.

'He certainly doesn't speak quietly,' he agreed. His expression quickly became serious again. 'What else did you hear?'

'I heard you tell him that you *would* marry one day and return, but only when the time was right. Then, when he asked you when that would be, I heard you tell him he had to be patient.'

'That's all? You didn't hear anything else?'

'No. That was enough.'

'Enough? For what, exactly?'

'It was enough to make me realise that I shouldn't delude myself that you'll ever want to have a serious relationship with *me*.'

'Is that really what you believe, Kit?' His brow furrowing in concern, Hal reached out a hand and curled it round her wrist. Then he pulled her towards him.

For a few moments she teetered, anxiously trying to regain her balance and not fall against him. But he was already winding his arms round her waist to steady her, and gazing up into her eyes as though he would never willingly tear his gaze away to look at anything else. At once the scent of his warm, virile body enveloped her and she knew that even if she could muster the most powerful will in the world she wouldn't be able to deny him anything that he desired if it gave him pleasure and made him happy.

'What am I to believe, if not that?'

'How about that I honestly want to have a serious relationship with you? That I'll go crazy if I can't have the one woman in the world who means more to me than anybody else?'

Every other thought in her head was obliterated at that heartfelt assertion. Sorrow seemed a million light years away when Hal looked at her the way he was looking at her now. As if she was something infinitely precious and he would willingly sacrifice everything he owned to keep her safe.

CHAPTER TWELVE

'I CAN HARDLY believe it,' Kit admitted softly.

'Well, you must—because it's the truth.'

Her handsome companion's voice was gravelly with emotion.

'You might travel to the ends of the earth, Kit Blessington, but wherever you go I swear I'll come and find you and bring you home.'

A warm surge of tears swam into her eyes. 'You mean it? You're not just saying that?'

Hal's handsome face was immediately perturbed. 'I might not always agree with everything you say or do when we're together, and I'm sure sometimes sparks will fly when I feel the need to hold my ground and you protest, but one thing I promise you: I will never lie to you about my feelings. You have my word on that.'

'What feelings are we talking about, Hal?' Right then it wouldn't have been difficult to convince Kit that she was dreaming. Having her wishes fulfilled had never happened very often, and more often than not she expected to be disappointed.

'Don't you know? Can't you guess? I thought I'd made it perfectly clear.'

It was hard to hear him over the sonorous thumping of her heart, let alone give herself permission to speculate. 'If it was so clear then I wouldn't need to ask, would I?'

Shaking his head, Hal bemusedly acceded to her tremulous suggestion. 'All right, then. I'll tell you.' His tawny, long-lashed eyes visibly darkened. 'I'm mad about you, Kit. To make it even clearer, so there's no possibility of confusion, I'm head-over-heels in love with you, and I'll happily spend the rest of my days showing you how much I mean that—mean it with all my heart.'

Kit stared at him in shock even as her heart leapt joyfully. 'You *really* love me? I mean—I know I'm not the type of girl you normally go for. I'm very ordinary. And I'm not just saying that because I'm fishing for compliments. I'm…I'm being realistic.'

'Well, maybe it's time you woke up to a new reality, Kit. One in which you start to realise how beautiful, sexy and desirable you truly are.'

She could still hardly believe what she was hearing. 'You know what? Not only do you have a worrying pre-dilection for dangerous sports, Henry Treverne, but I've come to realise that you're a very dangerous man too.'

'Hmm…why do you say that, I wonder?' His lips quirking in a gentle grin, he tenderly pushed away some coiled Titian strands from the side of her face and let his palm linger there, intermittently stroking the pad of his thumb down over her cheek.

Inside the sprigged cotton of her pretty pyjamas, the tips of Kit's breasts—already so acutely sensitive whenever he was near—tingled and hardened. They surged against the lightweight material, desperately seeking his touch.

'I say it because it's true—and the reason I find you dangerous is because I love you too. And when you love someone it inevitably makes you vulnerable. That's something I vowed I'd never allow myself to be when I left home, because life with my mother—the one person I loved more than anybody else—was such an emotional rollercoaster ride it was frightening. I longed for some stability for us both when I was young—a place that we could call our own. But it didn't happen. Because whenever my mum met someone and started to trust them they usually ended up breaking her heart and fleecing her of every penny. Then we'd have to move on again. I constantly lived in fear that something would happen to her when she was down and upset about a man because I saw how vulnerable it made her. So I decided not to risk the same thing happening to me. The last thing I expected to happen when I came to work for you was that I'd come to love you, Hal.'

The sense of wonder at his revelation that he reciprocated her feelings couldn't prevent her still being anxious about the pain she'd suffer if anything ever happened to him—or, worse still, if he should ever leave her. But realising that was just old programming kicking in, because she'd grown up fearing that if she got involved with a man he would behave in the same destructive way as her mother's various unreliable boyfriends, Kit knew she had to trust that her own path was more hopeful. But she still wanted to come clean about her fears to Hal.

'I've guarded my heart against falling in love for so long because I've had no good example of a man being sincere or keeping his word, and I witnessed the devastation that caused my mum. I was determined not to repeat it. But nothing could have prepared me for a man like you, Hal.' She smiled. 'Or the effect that you would have on me. I found myself dangerously fascinated by you almost straight away, and that feeling has grown stronger. So much so that I can't be remotely sensible about what's the best course of action for me any more.'

'What kind of action does your *heart* want you to take?' Hal prompted, his tawny eyes turning to a deeply hypnotic liquid gold that silently and irrefutably conveyed how aroused he was.

Unable to deny her need to touch him intimately any longer, Kit slid her hand round the back of his neck and slowly brought his face towards hers.

'My heart tells me to kiss you until I'm drunk with the taste and flavour of you. Until it beats in tandem with yours. God knows I've tried, but I just can't seem to resist you. But I'm sure you know that already, don't you?'

'I don't take anything for granted where you're concerned, baby, but I was hoping you'd say that. And I want you to know that I'm so sorry you had such a rough time of it growing up. But that time is past. And if it's a place of your own that you want, then I'll get it for you. I'm no psychic, sweetheart, but I can tell you right now that your future is looking much brighter.'

Even though his loving words thrilled her, and reassured her that he understood her need for a place that she could call her own, Kit couldn't totally dispense with her anxiety about it. 'I—I don't just want a place of my own any more, Hal,' she said softly. 'I don't care where I live so long as I can be with you. Is that—is that possible, do you think?'

'Is it *possible*? Surely you know by now that's what I want too?'

Even before he crushed her lips beneath his Hal was expertly undoing Kit's buttons and sliding his hands inside the material of her pyjamas to cup her breasts. Then as their kiss deepened, with both their mouths opening hungrily to accommodate the other's searching tongue, his fingers tugged on the aching steel buds of her nipples to inflame them even more. If Kit thought anything at all in those incendiary few seconds, it was about for how long and how passionately he would pleasure her. In turn, would she be able to repay *him* with equal pleasure?

She needn't have worried. Proving he was as instinctive a lover as she could wish for, Hal's fingers and thumbs started to ease her pyjama bottoms down over her svelte hips. As soon as he'd done so his hand returned to slide between her silken thighs and stroke over the sensitive bud at her moist centre.

Trembling with anticipation, Kit tore her lips away from his and dropped her head down onto his iron-hard shoulder. She'd had no idea that such staggering gratification was even possible until she'd fallen in love with this man. 'Hal, please...' she couldn't help her voice breaking with need.

'There's no need to beg me for anything, baby,' he responded huskily. 'I know what you want and I know what you need. I know it because I feel the same. I want you so much that I think I'll die if I can't have you.'

He was kissing the smooth skin on her neck and nibbling it at the same time. Then in one smooth movement he lay back on the bed and, with his hands firmly on her hips, eased her body over his.

'I don't want you to die,' Kit breathed, her hands fumbling at the fly of his jeans and tugging them down as carefully as she could over his strong, muscular thighs. Her blood palpably thrummed, because the need to feel his possession suddenly grew urgent.

Hal didn't hesitate to oblige her. Shoving aside his black silk boxer shorts, he plunged his hardened silken shaft deep inside her and, lifting his hips, pressed upwards. Before, his persistent taps at her door had rendered her terrified, in case it was the precursor to a ghostly visitation, but now Kit's full-throated cries of pleasure echoed uninhibitedly round the room instead, banishing any sense of sadness and regret that it might previously have held.

If their loving had anything to do with it, from now on she knew that it would be passion and joy that the bricks and mortar here were imbued with. And as heady desire enslaved them, guaranteeing they would be seductively preoccupied long into the night, the forceful storm of their loving shut out every memory of past hurt and disappointment that might have haunted them, ensuring the future was suddenly not half so fearful as they might once have imagined.

Just before the dawn broke Kit fell asleep in Hal's arms. There was no question that she would do anything else. All self-doubt had fled. It had been replaced by calm, assured surrender to whatever came next. As long as they were together she knew she could face any adversity or sorrow and overcome it. That was what love did, she realised. It made you strong, *not* weak. All these years she'd been labouring under a cruel misconception. What was the point of living if you never experienced loving someone? If you were so afraid of being hurt that you never trusted the wisdom of your own heart? Searching for guarantees and trying to work it all out in your head, clearly wasn't the answer. Decisions should be made out of love, not fear. From now on, Kit vowed, that would be her mantra.

When she woke a few hours later her eyes opened to find Hal examining her thoughtfully, casually resting back on his elbow as he gazed down at her. His arresting golden eyes, hard chiselled jaw and curling tousled hair was definitely a sight she would never tire of waking up to.

'Are you all right?' she asked, suddenly afraid that he might have needed her but had decided against disturbing her to let her know.

'I'm fine. In fact I'm *more* than fine. I feel on top of the world. I've just been lying here wondering how on earth I've had the good fortune to attract someone as good and beautiful as you into my life.'

It wasn't easy for Kit to keep her humour at bay. 'Good fortune? Some people might think that the circumstances were a disaster. You broke your leg, remember? I suspect that had something to do with it.'

He scowled, gathered a coil of her russet hair between his fingers and for a few seconds examined it intently. 'I confess I was expecting a much more romantic reply than that, sweetheart. It's all well and good that one of your qualities is that you're eminently sensible and pragmatic, but I'd like to know that you can be dreamy and romantic too.'

She hastened to reassure him. 'I promise you I can. It's just that it's become rather a habit of mine to be sensible. In future one of the things I want to achieve is an ability to give myself permission to enjoy life more—to have fun and be silly if I want to and not worry about looking a fool.'

'I'm glad to hear it. But you could never look like a fool, Kit. Talking of achieving things—do you remember when you came into my study and asked if there was anything else I'd like to achieve, other than all the business awards and sporting accolades displayed round the room?'

She nodded. 'I do. As I recall, you said there *were* other things you'd like to achieve, and it did make me think.'

'There's not much you don't remember, is there? I'll have to watch out in the future if I dare forget your birthday or what kind of flowers you like. I'll definitely be in the doghouse if I do.' Grinning, Hal reached for her hand, then raised it to his lips and planted a kiss. 'Well, to expand on that comment, the one thing I want to achieve above everything else is to find the woman of my dreams, marry her, then settle down to have a family.'

As Kit all but held her breath his golden-eyed gaze deepened meaningfully.

'To that end, I'm asking you to marry me, Kit.'

She immediately sat up and stared at him. 'You're being serious?'

'I most certainly am. And, trust me, this moment will be imprinted on my memory for many years to come.' Disconcertingly, he chuckled. 'Not just because it's one of the most momentous occasions of my life, but because I won't be able to forget what you were wearing when I proposed.'

'What I'm wearing? But I'm—' Stricken with embarrassment, Kit realised she was naked. Her sensible pyjamas had long been dispensed with during the night. She made a grab for the counterpane and held it firmly over her breasts.

'Naked!' Hal finished for her, unrepentantly wrenching the counterpane back and giving her a lascivious smile. 'And that's just the way I want you. Because when you've given me your answer—and I'm hoping it's the one I want to hear…' He paused to deliver a tantalising little kiss on her mouth and then teasingly caught her lip between his teeth for a moment. 'I intend to shut out the world for the rest of the day…' another sizzling kiss was dropped at the satin juncture of her neck and shoulder '…and make wild, passionate love to you.'

It was difficult for Kit to comment because she was so stunned. Shyly, she determinedly freed the silk counterpane from his grip and tugged it back up over her breasts. 'I'm far from against the idea, but you're not supposed to overdo things, remember? We've already been up most of the night and… Exactly *how* wildly passionate are you intending to be?'

'That's for me to know and you to find out, angel. Now, stop wasting time worrying about me overdoing things, shut up, and let me propose again…but properly this time.'

Kit lost any inclination to argue. Keeping quiet was suddenly not such a challenge after all.

Pushing back his tousled dark hair, Hal made his handsome face assume a serious expression.

'Katherine Blessington, will you do me the honour of becoming my wife and making me happy…*far* happier than any man has a right to hope to be on this earth?'

'Yes, Henry Treverne, I will. I'll marry you. Because

I can't imagine ever living without you and I love you much more than words could ever say. But I still won't stop trying to find the right ones to tell you.'

His strong arms enveloped her then, and there was a magical sense of time standing still. It wasn't just Hal who would remember these precious moments forever. *Kit would hold them in her heart until the day she died.*

A sudden sharp knock at the door made her gasp. Her pulse raced in shock. It raced even more when Hal's father's resonant voice enquired loudly, 'Hal? Are you and Ms Blessington ready for a cooked breakfast? I thought we could all have it in the dining room this morning, and Mary tells me it's going to be ready in about twenty minutes. Does that give you both enough time to shower and dress?'

Shaking his head in amusement, and hardly looking at all surprised, Hal answered, 'Make it half an hour and we'll be there on the dot. Thanks, Dad!'

'Don't mention it. It's nice to have you home, son.'

Sir Henry's receding footsteps echoed clearly round the room as he made his way back down the stone flags of the corridor.

'Your father sounded like he knew you were in here with me.' Kit's blue eyes widened in disbelief. 'How could he *possibly* know that?'

'I told him last night that I was going to pay you a visit and propose to you. Turns out he didn't have to be so patient in waiting for an answer as to when I'd marry and return home after all.'

'You mean—you mean you *discussed* the fact that you love me and want to marry me? What did he say? Was he surprised? I don't expect he was very happy.

I'm sure he must believe you could do a whole lot better for yourself than me. Tell me, Hal—was he angry?'

'Stop doubting and torturing yourself, will you? Of *course* he wasn't angry. My father knows how lucky I am to have found you, and he certainly doesn't think I could do any better. Class isn't such an issue nowadays—and nor should it be when two people fall in love. And I'm no Prince Charming, devoid of any faults, so don't kid yourself that I am, Kit. It's *me* who's the lucky one in this relationship. And the only thing my dad wants to be assured of is that I'm with someone I love, who loves me. He was as pleased as punch when I told him how I felt about you. He said he knew you were something special the moment he set eyes on you. Apparently my sister confirmed it for him. She talks to him on the phone at least once a day and she spoke very highly of you.'

'All right, then. You've convinced me.'

'Where are you going?'

Having thrown back the covers, Kit was hurriedly stepping into her pyjama bottoms and reaching for the top half that lay discarded on the counterpane. Her hair tumbled in a riot of burnished copper waves down over her slim pale shoulders and alluring naked breasts and Hal thought she resembled an enchanting elfin sprite from one of his and Sam's childhood fairy stories— but a very *sexy* red-haired sprite. He almost wanted to pinch himself, to check he wasn't dreaming that she'd agreed to marry him.

'I'm going to go and take a shower and then get dressed. I don't know about you, but I'm not going to turn down the offer of a cooked breakfast any time soon. When I'm done I'll come and help you.'

Hal couldn't help releasing a very audible curse and, echoing his frustration, his injured leg began to throb. 'It's bad enough that I have to endure the thought of you showering naked on your own when I want to join you. There's not much I can do about that…but then to suffer the indignity of you looking at me with those big baby-blue eyes like I'm some poor helpless invalid…' He cursed again and impatiently scraped his hair back off his forehead. 'You have no idea what I'd give to be able to get up and carry you into that blasted shower myself!'

'You're wrong, Hal.'

Her voice was more tenderly compassionate than he'd ever heard it before, and Kit returned to his side of the bed and carefully sat down.

Taking his hand in between hers, she said, 'I know how much it tears at your self-esteem and your pride that you can't do all the things you did with ease before the accident. But, honestly, with all the progress you're making it will be no time at all before you're walking around again, fully fit, *and* chasing me round the kitchen for a kiss to boot!'

'And joining you in the shower?' Despite the flash of irritability and frustration that had seized him, Kit's calm-voiced reassurance had done a lot to alleviate Hal's concerns. With pleasure, he saw that she was blushing too.

'I'll look forward to it,' she said, and smiled.

'Well, I suppose you'd better go and get ready. We shouldn't let that cooked breakfast go to waste, should we?'

'Are you kidding? Something tells me I'm going to need to eat all the cooked breakfasts I can get to build up my strength if I'm to meet your insatiable demands, Hal Treverne.'

Dropping a kiss on the side of his cheek, she got to her feet and disappeared into the bathroom…

EPILOGUE

One year later

KNOWING THAT HER adventurous husband was champing
at the bit to be off on the most taxing mountaineering
hike he'd undertaken since his leg had fully healed—
this time on Ben Nevis, the highest mountain in Britain—Kit hesitated outside the stately bedroom in the
private wing they'd made their home in at Falteringham House.

They'd moved in shortly after they'd married because
Hal had decided it was time he came back to his ancestral home and learned the ropes of running the estate
with his father. Kit had agreed. Although it wasn't easy,
getting used to living in such a grand place, she was
definitely adapting to it and had been delighted when
her father-in-law, Sir Henry, had asked if she'd like to
take over the PR aspects of running the estate. She'd
taken to the job like a fish to water.

But now Hal was busy packing his gear to head off
to Ben Nevis, and she couldn't help anxiously biting
down on her lip at the thought of the adventure he had
ahead of him. He would only be gone for the weekend,
but any separation from him had to be endured always

seemed like purgatory to Kit. Sometimes she would swear that they were literally two halves of the same soul, and even after nearly a year's marriage their need for each other seemed to grow even greater, *not* lessen. However, she had promised him on their wedding day that she would never seek to curtail the sports and adventures that gave him pleasure just because she was fearful of the danger he might put himself in. Hal was a loving and devoted husband, and challenging himself was part of who he was. Kit wouldn't want him to be any different.

But maybe today she had good reason to revise that view...

Lifting her hand and briefly sucking in a steadying breath, she rapped on the walnut door. 'Hal? I know you're busy, but can I come in for a minute?'

No sooner had she finished speaking than he opened the door, and just as though she'd been brought face to face with his six-foot-two, straight-legged frame for the very first time her heart skipped a beat. He was wearing faded jeans and a dark blue chambray shirt, and his tawny chameleon eyes glinted with pleasure as soon as they alighted on his wife's face.

Straight away his arms encircled her waist to bring her close against him. 'Since when do you need to knock on the door to ask if you can come in? This is your bedroom too, sweetheart.'

'I know.' She smiled, but her voice was perhaps not as steady as she would have liked it to be. 'I just thought I'd see how you were getting on with your packing and if you needed any help.'

'You can't resist offering to help me, can you?' Hal lowered his head to brush his warm lips tenderly across his wife's. 'I know you mean well, angel, but I've been climbing and hiking long enough over the years to know the drill for how to pack and what to take.' His smooth brow puckered for a moment. 'But that's not it, is it? I mean that's not the reason you wanted to come in and talk to me? Is everything okay? I know you've been feeling a little under par since we came back from our trip to Morocco a few weeks ago. Do you think it's something you ate that's caused it?'

'No, Hal, I don't think I've been under par because of something I ate.' Apprehensively Kit lifted her gaze to his. 'I've just found out that I'm pregnant.'

'What?' His expression was so shocked it was almost comical.

'I'm pregnant.'

'How do you know? Have you been to see a doctor?'

Her stomach plunged at the uncertainty in her husband's tone. 'Don't you believe me?'

'If you tell me it's true then of course I believe you—but how do you know you haven't made a mistake? That it's not just some kind of tummy bug? I've heard there's one going round...'

'I bought a pregnancy test and it was positive. I'm going to have a baby, Hal. Do you mind? I know the news probably could have come at a more conducive time, seeing as you're about to make your first mountaineering trip since the accident, but I hoped it might make you determined to be extra careful when you're up on that mountain and to come home to me just as soon as you can so that we can celebrate.'

'I'm going to be a father... We're going to be *parents*!'

Lifting her high into his arms, Hal hugged her hard

and swung her round in a circle with delight. Then he kissed her hungrily and passionately until she had to push against him to let her up for air. Dizzy with relief that he shared her joy that they were going to have a child, Kit cupped Hal's chiselled jaw and smiled tenderly up into his eyes—eyes she now knew she'd lost her heart to from the very first glance.

'I'm so glad that you're pleased about it, Hal. For a moment there I was afraid you might not be.'

He gave her a bemused look. 'Why on earth would you think that? I told you on the day I asked you to marry me that it was what I wanted most in the world—to marry the woman of my dreams and settle down and have a family. Don't you remember?'

Kit sighed as Hal delivered her safely to the ground again. 'I remember. But I don't want you to settle down, my love. It's never going to be in your nature to just be content with raising a family—and that's not a criticism. I know you have to run the estate, but that's no reason not to do the things you love as well...the sports and the challenges that give you pleasure. As long as you promise not to take too many unnecessary risks—because I want you to come home in one piece to me and our children—then that's fine by me. You wouldn't be the adventurous and brave man I married if I tried to change you in any way. I love you just as you are, Hal Treverne.'

'And I adore you, Katherine Treverne. And I promise that from now on I will never take any dangerous risks that I don't have to. You and our children will always be the most important things to me in the world. And talking of celebrating our good news...I don't have to

leave for Ben Nevis for a while yet, so why don't we
start our celebrations early?'

He was already lightly pushing her towards the vast
king-sized bed that they shared and Kit didn't have a
single thought in her head to protest, no matter how
'under par' she felt.

Hal and their marriage meant everything in the world
to her, and for as long as they lived she would happily
take every opportunity she could to let him know it.

* * * * *

A sneaky peek at next month...

MODERN™

INTERNATIONAL AFFAIRS, SEDUCTION & PASSION GUARANTEED

My wish list for next month's titles...

In stores from 17th January 2014:

❑ A Bargain with the Enemy – Carole Mortimer

❑ Shamed in the Sands – Sharon Kendrick

❑ When Falcone's World Stops Turning – Abby Green

❑ An Exquisite Challenge – Jennifer Hayward

In stores from 7th February 2014:

❑ A Secret Until Now – Kim Lawrence

❑ Seduction Never Lies – Sara Craven

❑ Securing the Greek's Legacy – Julia James

❑ A Debt Paid in Passion – Dani Collins

Available at WHSmith, Tesco, Asda, Eason, Amazon and Apple

Just can't wait?

Visit us Online

You can buy our books online a month before they hit the shops! **www.millsandboon.co.uk**

0114/01

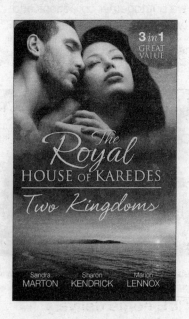

Join the Mills & Boon Book Club

Subscribe to **Modern**™ today for 3, 6 or 12 months and you could **save over £40!**

We'll also treat you to these fabulous extras:

- 🌹 **FREE L'Occitane gift set worth £10**
- 🌹 **FREE home delivery**
- 🌹 **Rewards scheme, exclusive offers…and much more!**

Subscribe now and save over £40
www.millsandboon.co.uk/subscribeme

The World of Mills & Boon®

There's a Mills & Boon® series that's perfect for you. We publish ten series and, with new titles every month, you never have to wait long for your favourite to come along.

Blaze®

Scorching hot, sexy reads
4 new stories every month

By Request

Relive the romance with the best of the best
9 new stories every month

Cherish™

Romance to melt the heart every time
12 new stories every month

Desire™

Passionate and dramatic love stories
8 new stories every month

Discover more romance at

www.millsandboon.co.uk

- ❤ WIN great prizes in our exclusive competitions

- ❤ BUY new titles before they hit the shops

- ❤ BROWSE new books and REVIEW your favourites

- ❤ SAVE on new books with the Mills & Boon® Bookclub™

- ❤ DISCOVER new authors

PLUS, to chat about your favourite reads, get the latest news and find special offers:

- 📘 Find us on facebook.com/millsandboon

- 🐦 Follow us on twitter.com/millsandboonuk

- ❤ Sign up to our newsletter at millsandboon.co.uk